SNOW AT 5 PM

SNOW AT 5 PM

Translations of an Insignificant Japanese Poet

by

JEE LEONG KOH

Commentary by Sam Fujimoto-Mayer

SNOW AT 5 PM
Copyright © 2020 Jee Leong Koh

Published by Bench Press,
an imprint of Gaudy Boy LLC
www.singaporeunbound.org/gaudyboy

Cover design by Guy E. Humphrey
Cover mechanical design by Mona Lin
Interior design by Jennifer Houle

ISBN 978-0-9994514-1-0

Some of the haiku and commentaries have been published in *Alba, Almost Island, Ambit, Assaracus, The Capilano Review, Dusie, From Walden to Woodlands, Gulf Coast, Haikuist Network, Hayden's Ferry, Kin, Literary Matters, Long Poem Magazine, Rattle, Queer Southeast Asia,* and *Ten Thirty.*

Permission information for previously published material is on pages 379–384.

In memory of Jin Hirata (1972–2016)

"*I dedicate this work to the USA, that it become just another part of the world, no more, no less.*"

—JOHN CAGE, LECTURE ON THE WEATHER

SNOW AT 5 PM

Sam Fujimoto-Mayer's Family Tree

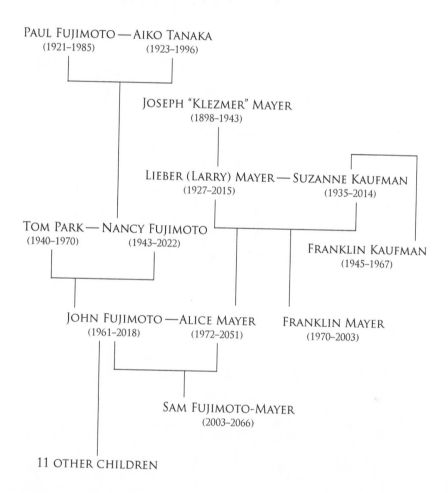

Paul Fujimoto — Aiko Tanaka
(1921–1985)   (1923–1996)

Joseph "Klezmer" Mayer
(1898–1943)

Lieber (Larry) Mayer — Suzanne Kaufman
(1927–2015)   (1935–2014)

Tom Park — Nancy Fujimoto
(1940–1970)   (1943–2022)

Franklin Kaufman
(1945–1967)

John Fujimoto — Alice Mayer
(1961–2018)   (1972–2051)

Franklin Mayer
(1970–2003)

Sam Fujimoto-Mayer
(2003–2066)

11 other children

PREFACE

It has been fifty years since the publication of *Snow at 5 PM*, and the slim volume continues to expand in light and darkness. The light comes from the growing recognition of the astonishing quality of the haiku. Leading critics have compared the poems favorably with the best of Buson and Issa and placed them within the fragrant shade of Bashō. The foremost haiku scholar of our day, Yamamoto Kenkichi-san of Tokyo University, who had held out against the tide of opinion, finally added his voice to the swelling chorus. In the esteemed journal *Frogspawn*, he judged the poetry to be of "the highest order."

What makes these haiku so distinctive? The short answer is that, like the Torah, each and every verse displays a thousand glittering aspects. According to its historical situation, each generation grasps one aspect of the truth. In our generation, *Snow* reveals itself to be concerned with the cultivation of a radical impulse. The seasonal cycle of a haiku collection must not mislead us into thinking that the verse form is always and essentially routinizing. Neither must the Zen spirit that animates the haiku tradition make us focus solely on interiority. Instead, *Snow* is politically revolutionary for our times. Each and every verse must be uncovered and explained with reference to social justice.

The expanding darkness has, of course, to do with the mystery of the author's identity. The poems have been scrutinized for clues from many different directions—post-structural, psychogenic, piscatorial, painful. Innumerable hypotheses have been advanced based on the flimsiest, but newest, thought. The most intriguing speculations make use of the latest research methodologies. Armed with the biggest database of poetry ever assembled, Professor Yi-Fen Chou at Columbia University deployed computer modeling of recurring tropes to show a very strong link to the writings of the utopian traveler William Guest. No one has, however, proven that Guest knew Japanese. Alexander Pichushkin, visiting scholar at Harvard—not the serial killer who wished to hammer open the skulls of sixty-four people, the same number of squares on his beloved chessboard—has proposed a line of thinking analogous to the postmortem analysis of chess games. This would require two poets to play opposing roles while contemplating the dizzying combinatorial possibilities of the haiku.

The fact that the poems are in English translation, that the Japanese originals are missing, further complicates the search. We are at the mercy of the inexact art of translation, let alone the skill of the translator. Jee Leong Koh, the translator of *Snow*, is the subject of a busy secondary industry. Koh discovered the half-destroyed manuscript when he moved into his Upper West Side apartment in New York City in 2011. He proceeded to translate the haiku and published them himself. Like so many writers before and after him, Koh moved from elsewhere, in his case Singapore to New York, in search of immortal fame and, like so many before and after him, achieved a temporary notoriety. He died choking on a sausage, egg, and cheese sandwich on an everything bagel. No one was around in the Brooklyn neighborhood of Bushwick at the wee hours of the morning to perform the Heimlich. Gone with the wind was any information about the manuscript. We have only Koh's patently uninformative note to go on.

The lack of information provides a fertile field for nonsense. The Singapore school of criticism recently argued that there is no Japanese-language author, that in fact Koh wrote the haiku in English and passed them off, for reasons best known to him, as translations. The school (and they are a school for they are tremendously well financed and trained, regimental we may say if we are inclined to be uncharitable) points to the fact that no Japanese originals were published alongside the English translations, as evidence for their specious claim. Only the translator could vouch for the existence of a Japanese manuscript. The school argues further that Koh was in the habit of writing poems as if translating from another language and points to an obscure poetic sequence called "Translations of an Unknown Mexican Poet" as proof. Putting aside the obvious objection that one sequence does not form a habit, I think that the outrageous claim can be dismissed by this single but all-important consideration: nothing in Koh's corpus of writings comes anywhere close to the poetic sublimity of *Snow at 5 PM*. The private-school teacher remained a majorly minor poet to the end of his life. It is not surprising that a young but imperious school of criticism, such as Singapore's, should mistake ambition, both the writer's and the critics', for authority.

Many commentaries on the poems have been published since the first appearance of *Snow*. They may be broadly classified as "aboveground" and "underground." Into the first category go commentaries that neutralize the revolutionary potential of these haiku by providing supposedly objective and scholarly, in a word, authoritarian, readings. They make these haiku suitable for study in book clubs and educational institutions. They are promoted by commercial interests and supported by the state. Provided free on the Internet, they are designed to capture the private information of users and flag their public discontent. The most popular commentary of this aboveground character is by the fraud, Konrad Boguslawski, an expatriate writer of the most bloated prose and critic of the cheapest shot from Russia, whose tiresome meddling in the study of American literature, like his government in our elections, has had the direst consequences for our democracy.

In the second category are the commentaries that circulate secretly, our American *samizdat*. These are written and copied out painstakingly by hand to prevent detection by electronic surveillance. The finest examples are *Snow on Snow* by Helen Snow and *What Father Does Not Say* by Ryhen Lovable. Arthur Arthur's work *Hermeticism and Haiku*, written in the form of a dialogue, is discredited by aboveground scholars, but its original take on the aesthetico-eroticism of these *koto no ha* (leaves of words) is highly stimulating. I owe these commentators a great debt for writing with such countercultural passion. It is a pity that I cannot reveal the true identities of these people to thank them properly but can only provide you with their pseudonyms.

On the fiftieth anniversary of the publication of *Snow*, I humbly offer my own notations, a labor of love over the course of a long and eventful life. I was thirteen years old when the volume first appeared in 2016, and I still remember the shock of recognition it afforded me as I perused its contents as a fifteen-year-old with vague poetic pretensions in Vinny's Barber Shop. While Vinny himself was gripping all so lightly my tender skull with his thick but well-manicured fingers, the poetic revelation came with the force of the first experience of sex—the fumble of understanding, the sweet intuitions. The thin book, with covers that were yellow, first by design, and then by age, has kept me company from Cincinnati, Ohio—the birthplace of American Reform Judaism and so much else—to Stanford University, where I studied comparative literature before dropping out, and finally to New York City, which has been my home and shelter for the past forty-odd years.

New York City has undergone great changes during that time. The author of *Snow* will not recognize his beloved Central Park. Because of chronic water shortages, watchtowers with oscillating guns now guard the reservoir against the tenements of lower Manhattan. The less adaptable flora, including the poet's favorite forsythia, have given up their ghosts to rising temperatures. Fleeing the floods, Wall Street now occupies Harlem. The so-called New Civil Rights Movement has succeeded in catapulting selected colored and transgender persons over the walls and keeping the huddled masses out. Where I am held, high above Hell's Kitchen, I can see Central Park (the zoo is gone), but I can no longer enter it. This commentary is offered as a way of preserving the park as a public commons, if not in actuality, then in the imagination.

Sam Fujimoto-Mayer
New York City
July 10, 2066

NOTE ON THE TRANSLATION

In January 2011, when I moved into my apartment on the Upper West Side, I found a slightly burnt sheaf of papers in the red-marble fireplace. Someone had done a poor job of burning the papers, out of hurry or reluctance.

What I gathered up was a bundle of haiku, composed in Japanese, written out by a graceful hand. To my further surprise, the poet made several allusions to Central Park, only a block away. I was thus compelled to translate the poems.

As I worked on the exhilarating, enigmatic pieces, I found myself searching out the street corner, the tree, and even the bird that had so enraptured our poet.

In this manner I traced the route taken through the Park—entering at 86th Street on the west side, then running south of the reservoir, or else strolling north of the Great Lawn by the Arthur Ross Pinetum, and finally exiting on the east side at either 84th or 85th Street.

Slowly I was beginning to live the life glimpsed through these haiku. I now walk in the poet's footsteps every day to where I teach school.

The manuscript had a title "ぐらつく," or "Unsettled," which has been crossed out firmly with three pencil strokes. I take the deletion as the author's intention, and so I have given this book a title by quoting the last line of the last haiku.

He or she signed off as "an insignificant Japanese poet."

Jee Leong Koh
New York City
January 31, 2016

SNOW AT 5 PM

Starlings singing
on the first day of spring
scratch a scratch

The American Acclimatization Society had a literary idea. They wished to introduce into America every bird mentioned in Shakespeare. In 1890, a member of the Society, German immigrant Eugene Schieffelin, released sixty starlings in Central Park. The birds soon multiplied and covered every part of the country, from coast to coast. Today they number 450 million, a bird for every person in the United States.

The sounds that starlings make are not beloved, to say the least. The singing, if it can be called that, is screechy, repetitive, and imitative. In fact, starlings appear only once in Shakespeare, in *Henry IV, Part 1*, where Hotspur considers their use as a way of tormenting the King. Literary critic Ichiro "Itchy" Yamada asks very properly, "Why does *Snow at 5 PM* begin with scratchy starlings?" His half-humorous self-reply: "Because they won't shut up."

Written 750 years before Schieffelin fired his feathered bullets, the Kuzari is a fictional dialogue in which a rabbi converts a pagan king to Judaism. In the seminal work, the author Judah Halevi compared prayers for the Restoration to "the chattering of the starling" since such prayers lacked whole-hearted desire. The diaspora did not really want to return to the Promised Land. Some, like my maternal grandmother, Suzanne Kaufman, feted as the Lily of New York, had built their lives, for many generations, in foreign soil and taken root—or, to change the metaphor, taken wing. So did Judah Halevi, a cultivated Andalusian Jew who spent his adult life in the world-loving cities of Toledo and Córdoba.

After he had finished composing the Kuzari in 1140, when he was in the middle of the north woods of his sixties, he made the extraordinary decision to undertake the dangerous journey across the Mediterranean to Israel, another kind of coast to coast. It was not enough for him to worship God where he was. It was . . . how shall

we put this . . . dictated to him that he should worship God in the land of his forefathers. We do not know if he reached his destination.

At the end of the Kuzari, the fictional rabbi makes a similar decision to travel to Israel over the protests of his royal convert. In the case of the rabbi, we do not ask whether he reaches the undiscovered country. That is the wrong literary question to ask. For if the German critic Theodor Adorno is right, and literature is the negative knowledge of the world—a view which had the most vehement opponent in my maternal grandfather, Larry Mayer, a.k.a. Lieber Mayer, who was liberated along with Elie Wiesel from Buchenwald by the 6th Armored Division of the United States Army—the philosophical rabbi is forever making his way to Israel, ever departing and ever arriving.

Sweet sweet sweet
rises from the swamp
into a yellow warbler

Unlike the starling, the yellow warbler is noted for its bright, sweet song. The genus name *Setophaga* comes from Ancient Greek: *ses* meaning "moth" and *phagos* meaning "eating." The specific name *petechia* comes from Italian and means "a small red spot on the skin." The liver steak, as my painter mother Alice Mayer would describe it, is found unanatomically on the breast.

The species, however, obeys Gloger's rule. German ornithologist Constantin Wilhelm Lambert Gloger was studying bird plumage from different climates when he observed that birds in more humid habitats tended to be darker than their relatives from more arid regions. One explanation for the phenomenon is the greater resistance of dark feathers to bacteria. Humid environments breed microbes more readily, and darker feathers are harder to break down.

The yellow warbler is certainly a strong adapter. It is, in the language of technology that we now favor, a first adopter, too. Its number in North America is remarkably stable because the bird favors second growth and luscious margins, and so it is not as vulnerable to habitat loss. It breeds in woods and thickets along the edges of streams, rivers, swamps, and marshes, in places that many other birds disdain.

In New York City, the warbler saw the transformation of swampland into Central Park beginning in 1858, after the razing of the free black settlement called Seneca Village, with its three churches, two schools, and two cemeteries. For two years, the village residents resisted the police but were finally evicted violently. The city government acquired all the private property through eminent domain. A stone outcrop near the 85th Street entrance on Central Park West is believed to be part of the foundation of the African Methodist Episcopal Zion Church.

According to our haiku, the yellow warbler still gives voice to the vanished swamp. But in what manner? A homely answer could be in

the manner of the morning whistle of my composer father John Fujimoto as he disappeared into his "studio" in the backyard to work on his "tunes." There he would stay, lost to the world and to me, until Alice could bear to look away from her easel and hurry down from the attic to throw a frozen dinner in the microwave and call him in.

A more philosophical answer must be sought elsewhere. I suggest that the warbler sings of the swamp in the manner of a quotation of the past. A quotation preserves the past while acknowledging the change (the smashing of altars, the splintering of chalkboards, the paving over of dead bodies). The philosopher Richard Rorty is perhaps relevant here.

Writing on the contingency of language, Rorty considers the process in which one language changes into another. It is difficult to specify some criteria but "roughly a break of this sort occurs when we start using 'translation' rather than 'explanation' in talking about geographical or chronological differences. This will happen when we find it handy to start mentioning words rather than using them—to highlight the difference between two sets of human practices by putting quotation marks around elements of those practices."

In other words, quotation = translation = change. There are unseen quotation marks around the yellow warbler's "Sweet sweet sweet," rising as it does from the vanished swamp, my parents' marriage, and the Japanese original.

A pin prick—
cardinal singing
in a bare tree

After two unremarkable, if intriguing, haiku, the third poem impresses by its surprising and apt juxtaposition of images. Tied together by the same color, red, a sensation and a song are synesthesized, suddenly.

Some commentators would not leave such poetic power alone but worry the poem for some deeper meaning. The Russian expatriate writer Konrad Boguslawski, for an instantaneous instance, insists on a sly chronological relation between the pin and the bird. In my mind's eye, I can still see him holding court among his acolytes, holding his pudgy figure as erect as Guryev porridge, pronouncing his tsarist and racist judgment that Asian American literature is all ("merely" is what he implies by his tone) about not belonging.

To illustrate his hypothesis about the haiku, he cooks up two stories. In the first story, a young girl is sewing a dress for a grand lady when she pricks her thumb. Angry at the undeserved suffering, she abandons the *jūnihitoe* for a walk outside, whereupon spotting a cardinal singing in a bare tree, she finds herself strangely consoled for the injury. The second story goes like this: a champion sumo wrestler undergoes a blood test, and the kiss of the needle brings him back to the village where he grew up as an orphan. His only friend then was a songbird, which died of a virulent cause one morning in its cage. The bird used to take food from his fingers.

We cannot deny the saccharine charm of both stories, but we must note the impoverishment to the haiku that they cause. They make of the haiku an allegory. The pin prick, the singing bird, they become plot devices and pale symbols. Chronology reduces the vivacity of the world. A narrative imposes too much order on reality. When we say a novel is poetic, we mean it is trying to escape the sweatshop and the cage bars of its genre.

With the sun
emerge the birdwatchers
I fluff

In *Fallout 15.3: A Post-Nuclear MMORPG*, a player can choose the role of the Chosen One, tasked by his starving village to find a Garden of Eden Creation Kit (GECK) to restore his community to prosperity. Traversing such locations in the bombed-out city as Carnegie Hall of Whores All Sexes and More, Heller's Cellar, and Diamond District, the Chosen One can opt to become a fluffer to survive in a postapocalyptic world of organized crime, slavery, and sex trade. This is to dive below in order to rise up. In his antinomian guises, he comes up against the Enclave, the remnant of the US government, which terrorizes inhabitants with its advanced technology and performs biological experiments on them. If the Chosen One is successful, he kills the POTUS and destroys the base of the Enclave on an offshore oilrig. The recovery of the GECK returns his village to lush life.

The game is not won, however, when the target is destroyed and the village is restored—it is not a straightforward narrative—but only when the space of its world-building, its unweeded garden, is wholly comprehended. Made up of different domains and dangers, actors and argots, it is only fully grasped through exhaustive repetition. After killing the President, a player may start the game again to find another way of doing away with Him, while navigating through Old Haarlem, South Street Spaceport, or the Midnight Garden of Good and Evil.

The video game made at the end of the last decade predicted our present desperation, with the Dataists, as the Israeli historian Yuval Noah Harari called them, in control, the electronic elite fucking us over and over. To see it another way, we are living in a simulacrum of our own making. Harari, whose middle name is proleptically prophetic, asked presciently, "Which of the two is really important, intelligence or consciousness?" We have consistently answered "intelligence" and so built our world. If you answer "consciousness" in the outmoded belief in

democratic equality, you are shown very quickly, and very electrically, how wrong you are.

What if, however, we decide to stop playing Harari's choice and instead take Hobson's gambit of leaving the game? To stop servicing the system and instead smash the game-set in hand? Will a new language emerge, a slogan more revolutionary than "I prefer not to"? I hear Boguslawski's explosive laughter in my ears, and his expletive "There is no escape from narrative." But the Squat Tsar would say that, wouldn't he?

Birdsong
a flash of lightning
in the ears

Growing up in America, in an artistic household certainly Cincinnatian in its quiet retirement from the lights of New York and its quirky readiness to sally forth on behalf of quixotic causes, I had absorbed the idea of poetry not only as a stay against confusion, but also as a mainstay against death. After God's demise, poetry is supposed to be our guarantee of an afterlife. This idea of poetry, ultimately derived from Europe, gives rise to the image of poetry as an immortal edifice.

The *locus classicus* of this thought is the Roman poet Quintus Horatius Flaccus. Horace, in short and in working shorts, wrote, "*Exegi monumentum aere perennius*," or "I have completed a monument more lasting than bronze" (to which a *Times Literary Supplement* reviewer appended the witticism: "although every word requires a scholar's note"). So Will Shakespeare wrote as if poetry would outlast brass, and stone, and earth, and boundless sea. So another Will, one W. B. Yeats, compared poetry to "monuments of unageing intellect."

But there is another way of viewing poetry, an ancient Japanese way, where poetry is an ephemeral and context-bound activity, where poems are exchanged—as in Lady Murasaki's *Genji monogatari*—between emperors and courtiers, priests and acolytes, lords and ladies, and are of the moment, "a flash of lightning / in the ears," as our poet puts it.

Our translator thought he found a manuscript of haiku discarded by the poet, or so his British education made him think. But what if the poems were not in the possession of the poet, but in the receipt of their intended recipient instead? In this alternative scenario, the poet did not live in that Upper West Side apartment but his correspondent did. He lived there for a time, and once a week, or more often, received a letter from our poet in which a haiku was enclosed. Did he keep all the haiku or only those that he particularly liked or partially

understood? When he had to move out of the apartment, why did he burn the haiku in the fireplace? Had he fallen out with our poet? Or lost interest in the haiku? Or was he trying to hide his association with the poet by destroying the incriminating evidence, the poet having committed an offense that was illegal, illiberal, even illegible, in the eyes of, respectively, the courts, the salon, and the university?

All this is to say that a poem is not the creation of an author only, but the joint creation of an author and a reader. No birdsong without the ears to hear it.

Birdcall in the spring—
squeaky
wheels

A humorous haiku.

In his commentary on *Snow*, Henry Ford—the literary critic, not the anti-Semite who turned out cars and underpaid workers in Detroit—brought to our attention an old saying: "the squeaky wheel gets the grease." The Chinese have a similar saying: "**会哭的孩子有奶吃**," which means, "The crying baby gets the milk." The Japanese are however more self-effacing, or conformist, depending on your view. The saying "The nail that stands out gets pounded down" (**出る釘は打たれる**, *deru kugi wa utareru*) is still widely used. The Koreans agree: "the pointy stone gets the chisel" (모난 돌이 정 맞는다).

A rare instance of agreement between the Japanese and the Koreans.

Spring wind
I can go left
or right

This haiku refreshes a common Zen or Taoist image of freedom from conceptualizations. It is of a family with these lines from a poem by the Tang Dynasty poet Hanshan (*Kanzan* in Japanese):

> No direction is better or worse,
> East just as good as West.
> Those who know the meaning of this
> are free to go where they want.
>
> (trans. Red Pine)

Hanshan, or Cold Mountain, who flourished in the ninth century, is a poet of mystery. His name is obviously a pseudonym. As to be expected, various scholars from the Humanities-Industrial Complex (a.k.a. HICX) have tried to identify him. The poet Gary Snyder, in my opinion, came closest to the truth about the author of the poems of liberation.

In an introduction to his translation, kept by my mother Alice on her Shiloh Mission nightstand and perused nightly with her piercing blue eyes, Snyder noted how with their wild hair and wilder laughter Hanshan and his buddy Shide (*Jittoku* in Japanese) were a great favorite subject of Zen painters. The pair became immortals, through their love of pranks perhaps, and, Snyder wrote, "you sometimes run into them today in the skidrows, orchards, hobo jungles, and logging camps of America."

Spring rain
in New York City
italicize

The Kierkegaardian distinction between a poetic and a religious response to nature is worth recalling here. According to Søren Aabye Kierkegaard, a poet and a Christian may both praise nature, but the former relates only imaginatively to nature whereas the latter strives existentially to learn from the lilies of the field and the birds of the air.

It is true that there is a *marked strain* of aestheticism in our haikuist's work, as in this example, which aligns our poet with Buson more than Bashō. Still, one can distinguish between imagination and existence too firmly and despair of our powers to regenerate a sense of purpose.

The spring rain in the haiku refreshes the gray city, home of The Gray Lady—I am referring not to the *New York Times*, but to my grandmother Suzanne, who could not be reconciled to her daughter's choice of career and consort *even by my birth* and so must remain indistinct and gray as washed-out newsprint—by reimagining coolness as *emphasis* and wetness as *difference*.

The typographical trope, so physically accurate in describing the tilt of rain, alludes wittily to New York City's status as the publishing navel of the world. The poem obeys in a life-enhancing manner *the Dickinsonian injunction* to "tell all the truth but tell it slant." [Transcriber's note: where SFM intended italics, he wrote in an exaggeratedly slanted hand.]

Spring morning
the averted eyes
of young girls

In *The Castle* by Franz Kafka, the villagers at the foot of Castle Hill tell the protagonist K., "We have a saying here that you may be familiar with: Official decisions are as shy as young girls." K. replied, "That's a sound observation, a sound observation. Decisions may have even other characteristics in common with girls."

On this passage, the German literary critic Walter Benjamin commented: "The most remarkable of these qualities is the willingness to lend oneself to anything, like the shy girls whom K. meets in *The Castle* and *The Trial*, girls who indulge in unchastity in the bosom of their family, as they would in a bed. He encounters them at every turn; the rest gives him as little trouble as the conquest of the barmaid."

Of K. and the barmaid, Kafka wrote with a fantastic fever that every gay boy in the 2020s coming from the boondocks to the Belvedere Castle of New York knew:

> They embraced each other; her little body burned in K.'s hands; in a state of unconsciousness which K. tried to master constantly but fruitlessly, they rolled a little way, hit Klamm's door with a thud, and then lay in the little puddles of beer and the other refuse that littered the floor. Hours passed . . . in which K. constantly had the feeling that he was losing his way or that he had wandered farther than anyone had ever wandered before, to a place where even the air had nothing in common with his native air, where all this strangeness might choke one, yet a place so insanely enchanting that one could not help but go on and lose oneself even further.

That is the "insanely enchanting" world of fantasy. The reality is too often "the averted eyes" of the haiku, the boy or girl in the bar or in the park, who will not give us the time of day. Yet these eyes give us

the power to see further into our real condition. They are, in fact, what Russian literary critic Viktor Shklovsky called "the estrangement device" (*priyom ostraneniya*) and what the German playwright Bertolt Brecht called, after Shklovsky, "the estrangement effect" (*Verfremdungseffekt*). Both *stran* in Russian and *fremd* in German share the same root, "strange."

The pale muscles
of young men
blameless in the sun

On the first warm day of spring, everyone used to be out in Central Park. Alone or in twos or threes, they stretched out cramped limbs on the Great Lawn, the men gladly taking off their shirts. The college man, having worked hard on his body the whole winter, threw a football to his equally muscular mate with a Tracy Bacon swagger that did the heart good to see. Even the pandemics could not keep them away, not permanently. They returned to showing off after the lockdowns had been lifted. Not anymore.

Spring morning
one suit says to another
be good

The meaning of this haiku was obscure until the brilliant critic Joe Kavalier suggested that the suits are not corporate types but comics superheroes, costumed in tights and underwear. As many have observed, including writers Michael Chabon and Maya Barzilai, the sons of Jewish immigrants from Russia and Eastern Europe created many of the superheroes in the golden age of comics, now still beloved by boys, and some girls, all over the world.

These second-generation immigrants, like Hananiah, Mishael, and Azariah of a past eon, also created themselves in the image of America by changing one name for another. Robert Kahn created Batman and Bob Kane. Stanley Martin Lieber created Spider-Man and Stan Lee. Hymie Simon created Captain America and Joe Simon. From the glaciated plains of Ohio, my home state, where he was born, Jerry Siegel created Superman, the granddaddy of this league of muscle Jews, and the golems Joe Carter and Jerry Ess.

My maternal grandfather, a contemporary of these super-Jews, kept his family name Mayer with its Hebrew meaning of "enlightenment" and its English evocation of an indecisive spring. He did, however, change his personal name from the mellifluous melody of Lieber to the popular acclaim of Larry. In other words, he went from beloved to laurel, from camp orphan to feted writer.

He was never as celebrated as Elie Wiesel, but he came close. He was Elie's Shadow, a superhero role never forgiven him by his peerless wife, the Lily of New York, who married him for his ghoulish glamor, not his gamesome gift. (Her true love was her Löwchen, which she named Penelope. "It's amazing," she said to all her friends, "she looked like a Penelope even when she was a pup.") His true bent was for mercurial comedy, laughter that hid a trapdoor under the rug.

For years, he considered committing his camp experience to the questionable shape of narrative and even showed me a few pages in his later years of the least harrowing incidents (I remember a comically imperfect hanging of a young boy), but when Wiesel's *Night*, sentimental and comestible, was brought out in America in 1956, Larry realized that the field belonged to the future Nobel laureate.

Opinion, the power that be, has kept shifting about the Jewish act of nominal change. In the comics creators' own assimilationist age, the change of names was applauded. It was deplored in the fin-de-siècle rise of identity politics. Our present moment, with its fascist ideologies, neoliberal economics, biotechnological revolutions, and quarky individualism, beholds the name-change with indifference. When you can modify the human genome, you cannot be too bothered by the alteration of names.

But like before, our current obsession with comic-book superheroes reflects the problems of our time, as Sam Clay elaborated long ago in his at once breathless and long-winded study *POW! WHOOSH! THUD!: The Poetics of Golden-Age Comics*. With all the superpowers at our disposal, we have no overpowering idea of how to "be good."

No smoking in the park
she tells her husband
beside the Lenten rose

The Lenten rose, also called the Christmas rose, is not a rose plant but a hellebore. A sturdy specimen of this perennial used to grow by the black walnut tree near the 85th Street entrance on the east side of the park. The misnaming of flora is rife in the history of the naming of flora (cf. my commentary on "Going incognito"). Before the Christmas of Adam's christening of the world, there was a Christmas Eve.

The first crocus
flashes its green card
at airport security

The haiku flaunts its audacity. It does not obey the traditional stricture against figurative language but breaks it instead by flashing a wildly inventive metaphor. It crosses the borders policed by generic ideas. It is here to stay.

We know now that its boldness is misplaced. Donald J. Trump was the first president to sign an executive order banning the reentry of green card holders into America if they came from a list of restricted countries. Although the ban was modified by popular protests, the precedent had been set for subsequent and wider bans to take effect, during the presidencies of the closeted Rear Admiral Randy McGill, the people's heiress Jenny C. Penny, and the former First Son and vapid movie star Barron Trump, in the name of protecting, first, the nation from terrorism, then the nation's jobs, and, finally, American pop culture.

The fight to open the borders has been led prominently by an alliance between Jewish and Japanese American organizations. In the fight, the name of Chiune "Sempo" Sugihara has often been invoked. Who was he? He was our man inside the Japanese embassy in German-occupied Lithuania during World War II, the disobedient bureaucrat. The story about this hero has been retold so often that it has acquired the status of myth. Here is my preferred version of the story.

Yukiko Sugihara had a dream. She dreamt that a man with ears tightly pressed to the sides of his head came up to her on a railway platform. He had no money for a ticket and would she, Yukiko, spare him some litai so that he could take the next train to Kobe? I'm leaving for Japan myself tomorrow, she heard herself saying, here, take this money for your fare. You know, don't you, that they only accept reichsmarks. The man took the two banknotes and thanked her earnestly. He hurried into the ticket office and disappeared from sight.

Then a woman, with a blond-haired girl in tow, who looked implausibly like Anne Frank, came up to her and asked for money for train tickets for her and her daughter. Yukiko opened her purse to show them it was empty and was surprised to find that it was not. There was just the right amount of reichsmarks for two tickets, although she could not say, after waking up from the dream, what the amount was.

After the woman left her, an elderly couple, he in a grease-stained monkey suit, she under a fish-oil-colored shawl, approached her. Yukiko looked up and saw a long line of people stretching down the train platform and disappearing into the forest. They were very orderly and very patient. They were full of an ancient respect for lawfulness that she recognized in herself. Each time she opened her purse, she found just the right amount of reichsmarks for each request. No matter how quickly she opened her purse, however, and emptied its contents to the man, woman, or child, the line never grew shorter. Its end never came in sight.

It was from this profound sorrow that she whimpered and woke up her husband Chiune. He, too, was having a restless night. He would get up and, in their few remaining days in Kaunas, write by hand six thousand visas for the Jewish refugees pouring into the city. At the end of each day, Yukiko would massage his swollen hands, red as the rose of her purse. When they finally made their way back to Japan, Chiune would be dismissed by his government for his disobedience of orders. The social disgrace was to come, but that night they held each other and wept.

Green shoots
new testament
of old roots

Christianity is a misquotation of Judaism, the New Testament a mistranslation of the Torah (cf. my commentary on "Sweet sweet sweet"). According to the Acts of the Apostles, the Church began with the Holy Spirit descending like tongues of fire and the followers of Christ speaking in foreign tongues and understanding one another perfectly. The Pentecostal miracle is presented as a marvel of perfect communication. The marvel is rooted in, routed by, an expressive mistake.

In his speech to the astonished followers, Simon Peter quoted the eighth verse of the sixteenth Psalm, "I foresaw the Lord always before my face," and explained that King David spoke "of the resurrection of Christ." But the Hebrew word *shiveh* does not mean "to foresee"; it means "to make level, to put, to set." King James's translators of the Old Testament knew this and translated Psalm 16:8 as "I have set the Lord always before me."

Rabbi Isaac M. Wise (1819–1900) was born in Steingrub, Moravia, and died in Cincinnati, Ohio, but not before building Plum Street Temple during the Civil War and founding the Hebrew Union College on Clifton Avenue in the same year as the passing of the Civil Rights Act prohibiting racial discrimination in public accommodations and jury duty. Whenever my mother was especially hard on her people, my father would bring up the name of the founder of American Reform Judaism, whose middle initial "M" stands for Mayer, also my mother's family name. My Japanese father, not my Jewish mother, was responsible for bicycling me to Plum Street Temple, renamed the Isaac M. Wise Temple but forever located on Plum Street, to hear the professional cantor sing on High Holidays.

Between the parentheses of his birth and death, Wise wrote many learned treatises defending Judaism against the fundamentalism of Christianity. On the King James Version quoted above, he concluded in *The Origin of Christianity: And a Commentary on the Acts of the*

Apostles (1868): "This translation, which is the correct one, does away altogether with Peter's assertion connected therewith, that David 'foresaw' the resurrection of Jesus."

Christian apologists have argued that under the inspiration of the Holy Ghostwriter, Peter did not mistranslate the Psalm so much as he retranslated it. He gave a divinely inspired turn to the words and made David prophesy of Christ. Not altogether excessively, Jewish defenders have described such a mistranslation as the new testament of a murdered Jewish king, priest, and poet.

All strong writing poses as the fulfillment of the past when it is, in fact, radically different. The scandal of the haiku is to expose the linguistic character of the natural world, and, by extension, that of religious faith. What do we call "green shoots"? What do we call "old roots"?

Hehe
drunk on shots
of forsythia

Brimming with color in their deep-lobed flowers, the forsythia shrubs along the reservoir path in Central Park were early heralds of spring. These sturdy, woody plants bloomed generously. Walking along the elevated dirt path, one could see the vehicular through-road running parallel but lower. The road was hemmed in on both sides by stone walls, but over the walls, forsythia poured its intoxicating ambrosia.

Helen Snow prefers to read "Hehe" as a simple, and musical, expression of individual delight. We may, however, wish to note an observation made by Arthur Arthur that "Hehe" is made up of two he's and so derive a picture of social conviviality. The literary observation goes well with my personal experience.

Going incognito
the forsythia drops
its medals

Native to East Asia, the forsythia was first entered into Western records by Swedish botanist Carl Peter Thunberg. As a white man confuses one ethnicity for another in an Asian bar, Thunberg categorized the forsythia wrongly as a lilac. He also thought that it was Japanese, but it was, in fact, Chinese originally.

The story of how Thunberg managed to enter Japan, closed to foreigners in 1775, is interesting. He was commissioned to visit the Dutch colonies and Japan to collect specimens for the Dutch botanical gardens. Stopping in Cape Town, Cape Colony, he stayed there for three years to learn Dutch in order to pass as a Dutchman since Japan was only open to Dutch merchants at the time, and even then they were confined to the small artificial island of Dejima, in the bay of Nagasaki.

Dejima was a small fan-shaped island formed by digging a canal through the peninsula. Its name means "Exit Island." Also living on the island incognito to the Japanese were Jewish merchants and explorers in the employment of the Dutch. In some ways, they can be compared to the seventy Jewish sages called to the island of Pharos, in the harbor of Alexandria, to translate the Torah from Hebrew into Greek. Legend has it that the translators working independently produced seventy translations in exactly the same words, thus testifying to the divine inspiration of the Septuagint. The spiritual descendants of these sages, the Jewish merchants of Dejima, translated themselves into Dutch men exactly and thus sanctified the divine inspiration of the Dutch commercial mission.

Thunberg was less divinely inspired. He was finally allowed to leave the island in mid-1776, when he accompanied the director of the Dutch settlement to pay respects to the shogun in Edo. One can imagine his intense excitement as he gathered never-before-seen

specimens on the slow journey and envisioned writing the book that
would bring him fame.

> Hollanders too
> have come for the blossoms—
> saddle a horse!

> (Bashō, trans. Makoto Ueda)

Thunberg published his book *Flora japonica* in 1784. It was rife with
errors. Many plants happily labeled as "japonica" came originally from
China. So eager to proclaim discovery, he had mistaken location for
locus classicus. The forsythia that Thunberg described as a lilac was
recognized later not to be a lilac. It was awarded its own genus and
named after Scotsman William Forsyth, the director of the royal gardens at Kensington at the time of the correction. The plant now bears
his name as a military uniform bears a medal.

In the forsythia
green is overtaking yellow
false positive

The fraud Konrad Boguslawski takes "false positive" as a self-apparent reference to the first HIV/AIDS pandemic and so dated the haiku to the 1980s. The desire to pin down the date of composition robs the haiku of its freshness. It seems, instead, to speak to all time. Right now, it speaks of the ascendancy of money, as in the green overtaking the yellow, and a summer that is false in the manner of a false dawn.

After the Republicans rolled back the Affordable Care Act, they took the anti-Asilomar action of removing all restrictions on genetic research. A private market soon developed, first on the dark web and then on the Clearnet, around the latest benefits of this research. To the highest bidder goes the ability to grow a third eye, usually at the back of the head, or to cancel out cancer. The annual reports of Aubrey de Grey, whose SENS Research Foundation is dedicated to finding a way for people to live up to a thousand, are parsed as if they are sutras or scriptures.

The arguments for giving children an "open future" are thrown out with the bath water. Parents want to give their children every genetic advantage they can afford. As part of this arms race, researchers are still trying to identify the homosexual gene in order to breed it out of existence, a project to which Boguslawski gives the green light of his assent.

The forsythia
overrun by its own leaves
a flag in tatters

Everyone knows that Allen Ginsberg read "Howl" at the Six Gallery in 1955. Less well known is the fact that Kenneth Rexroth presided over the reading. Dressed in a secondhand suit, he stepped up on a grape crate in front of the small crowd and declared that he was going to recite the *Iliad* in haiku form. This haiku has the flavor of what he recited that night.

Even less known is the attendance that night of one Kenji Kanno. He was visiting his friend Shigeyoshi "Shig" Murao, the clerk at City Lights Bookstore who was later arrested, along with Lawrence Ferlinghetti, for selling a copy of *Howl* to an undercover policeman. Shig and Kenji knew each other from Seattle, Washington. Both were incarcerated with their families during World War II and both were yes-yes boys, Shig joining Military Intelligence and serving as an interpreter in postwar Japan, Kenji fighting with distinction in the much-decorated 442nd Infantry Regiment in Italy.

To the question "Are you willing to serve in the armed forces of the United States on combat duty, wherever ordered?" in the so-called loyalty questionnaire, my great-grandfather Paul Fujimoto answered no. He was afraid that if he answered yes, the government would take him away from his wife and newborn daughter and send him to fight in the war. He was not sent to maximum-security Tule Lake camp along with other no-no boys but allowed to remain at Manzanar camp.

After my family was released from the camp, they tried to return to their fruit farm in California but faced so much hostility and discrimination from their neighbors, including fellow Japanese Americans, that they decided to move to Cincinnati, where no one knew them and where Paul's no continued to eat at him from the inside out.

After the war, Kenji Kanno returned to America with a flesh-eating wound in the thigh that would not heal. He had friends who had said

no, like my great-grandfather, but he did not hold it against them. Doctors kept amputating his limb a little at a time to try to save it, but the rot continued to spread upward. To spare his family the cycle of hope and anguish, Kenji faked death from the last surgery and took to the road, ending up in San Francisco. He would live for another two years after the Six Gallery reading.

What did he, a one-legged Japanese American veteran, think of the opening lines of "Howl"?

> I saw the best minds of my generation destroyed by madness,
> starving hysterical naked,
> dragging themselves through the negro streets at dawn look-
> ing for an angry fix . . .

Shig recorded in his diary that Kenji gave a slight smile, and smiled slightly again at these lines:

> who vanished into nowhere Zen New Jersey leaving a trail of
> ambiguous picture postcards of Atlantic City Hall,
> suffering Eastern sweats and Tangerian bone-grindings and
> migraines of China under junk-withdrawal in Newark's
> bleak furnished room . . .

What did Ginsberg know about Eastern sweats, Tangerian bone-grindings, migraines of China? Remember Kenji Kanno and his slight smile, O my readers, when you hear "Howl" again.

In the manila folder
the color of forsythia
a festival program

Wordplay holds the key to this haiku. Manila folders are so called because their cheap unbleached paper comes from Manila hemp. In Japanese, *mari*, a typographical twin to *mani*, can mean truth, long distance, village, but also hemp. Mari is, of course, the first name of the remarkable poet Mari Sasagawara. She is famous for writing, as her commentator Hisaye Yamamoto noted at the time, "the first published poem of a Japanese-American woman who is, at present, an evacuee from the West Coast making her home in a war relocation center in Arizona."

Erratically brilliant and tantalizing obscure, the long poem "The Dream of Forsythia" is about a man who makes Nirvana, or enlightenment, his lifelong goal. Determined to purge himself of worldly corruption, he pays no heed to the comings and goings of human desires in his daughter within the selfsame room, writes Sasagawara. She was my grandmother Nancy Fujimoto's favorite poet, and "The Dream of Forsythia" was her favorite poem. Growing up in Cincinnati, Nancy was confined to home, school, and the restaurant that her father, Paul, opened in Amberley Village.

The restaurant grew with the flight—fifteen minutes' drive, actually—of Jews from downtown Cincinnati. Every Christmas, when Christian shops piously closed, Fuji Sushi welcomed Father Abraham's hungry children, and again Nancy was stopped from joining her friends for the Holiday Party of the Year, missing the kissing, as her best friend Caroline Fuchs put it, and serving tables from morning to night. She was only fifteen minutes away from the time of her life, but she might as well have been an ocean away from the shore of romantic bliss. Naturally she conceived a lifelong hatred for the Jews.

The haiku compares the unenlightened desires of young women wittily to "a festival program." Suffice it to add that, whereas Sasagawara's

heroine has a forsythia-yellow folder, Nancy Fujimoto's folder was a delicate purple—*fuji* referring, or re-furring, not to the mountain but to the flowering wisteria. Sweets to the sweet.

The Singapore school of criticism has a more pedestrian explanation of the haiku. They note that Jee Leong Koh organized the first Singapore Literature Festival in NYC in 2014 and so would keep his festival plans in a folder of some kind. The fact that it is Manila, they claim, alludes to the Southeast Asian origins of the festival. I leave the reader to adjudicate which of the two explanations is more poetic.

Big dog sniffing
by the veiny tulip stalks
straining to pop

For the relationship between sex and enlightenment, one can do worse than look to the iconoclastic Zen monk poet Ikkyū Sōjun (1394–1481). Believing that his enlightenment is deepened by sexual intercourse, he would frequent brothels in his monk's black robe. Later in life, he fell in love with a blind singer named Mori, not Mari or Mani. He could write about her in the most direct, immediate, and moving manner, as in the following poem, written originally in the Chinese five-character style:

> My hand resembles Mori's hand.
> Yes, the master of loveplay,
> she cures the jaded stem.
> And my fellow monks rejoice.

Our haiku arguably transforms Ikkyū's stem to veiny tulip stalks about to burst into bloom. Enlightenment is not gradual but sudden, so our haikuist agrees with Zen practitioners and my grandmother Nancy.

Pale daffodils
poor wandering things
the souls of emperors

Inspired by Bashō, Japanese poet Yone Noguchi (1875–1947) embarked on his "tramp-journeys" from coast to coast, more specifically from San Francisco to New York City, writing of the natural landscapes on his way, such as Yosemite Valley, in a style reminiscent of Whitman's. Yone had literary ambitions: he wanted to make a name for himself.

In New York, boarding for a time on Riverside Drive, he met his editor and correspondent Léonie Gilmour and had a son with her. Léonie was not his only love. Yone was also a sexual wanderer who had romantic affairs with many younger literary women and intimate relationships with a number of older literary men, and he left Léonie to bring up their son on her own, just as my paternal grandfather did, when his time came.

Mother and son moved to Tokyo to be closer to the boy's father, but they did not see him overmuch. They moved to Omori and then to a seaside village called Chigasaki, on the eastern bank of the Sagami River, where the boy learned how to catch eels and to skin young willow twigs to make whistles. The future sculptor did receive a brave gift—his name Isamu—from his father when he first toddled into Japan. My grandfather did not name my father, so Grandma Nancy gave him the anonymous American name of John.

Of a Georgia O'Keefe painting of deep-blue petunias, Isamu Noguchi once said, admiringly, "That is nature as nature would do it." He would say the same of the daffodils in this haiku.

Konrad Boguslawski disagrees, however, and castigates the haiku for its cultural hybridity, calling it the miscegenated grandson of Emperors Marcus Aurelius and Hirohito. Against such genetic and literary fascists, we will quote Publius Ovidius Naso. Defending Homer's good name from his notorious critic, the pseudonymously

named Zoilus the Homeromastix ("Scourge of Homer"), Ovid shot back, "Spite disparages the genius of great Homer: that's where you get your name, Zoilus, whoever you are."

Two Japanese women
stop by the cherry tree
and remove their sunglasses

The Japanese word for staring hard at something, *mitsumeru*, has the more literal meaning of "packing yourself into seeing." This is absolutely right for appreciating the densely clustered blossoms of the cherry tree.

Two years before Yukio Ozaki, mayor of Tokyo, sent his cherry trees to the city of Washington, DC, five Japanese residents of New York City presented 2,500 cherry trees to their city in 1910. The donors were Kokichi Midzuno, Jōkichi Takamine, Rioichiro Arai, Daijiro Ushikubo, and Kikusaburo Fukui. The Washington trees were concentrated in one area, around the Tidal Basin. The New York trees were scattered across Upper Manhattan, including an annex to Riverside Park that was more like an appendix than a footnote, and subsequently renamed Sakura Park.

Milk and blood
the cherry tree holds up
without dripping

In 1912, in Sakura Park, five thousand people witnessed the unveiling of a large bronze tablet, which commemorated the gift of cherry trees to the city two years earlier. Representing the gift committee, Dr. Jōkichi Takamine "spoke in enthusiastic terms of the debt of gratitude which his country owed to the United States for first bringing to Japan the seeds of Occidental civilization," according to the *New York Times*.

Japanese Americans remember those seeds very well. We remember that Commodore Matthew C. Perry sent Japan a white flag with his final note of demand in 1853. We remember that President Harry S. Truman sent Japan two atomic bombs in 1945, on August 6 and 9, the first use of nuclear weapons in human history and, disastrously, not the last. We remember the man blown facedown, his back flayed to reveal muscle and bone. We remember the mother cradling her headless baby. We remember the woman wandering in a daze, her daughter's head in a bucket, among the debris. We remember the tests performed on *hibakushu* to gauge the effects of full-body radiation exposure so that we Americans could prepare for a nuclear attack on our own country. We remember General Douglas MacArthur sent Japan a new constitution, drafted in a week by children, disarming the country but arming Okinawa with American power, an occupation judged so successful that we would try the same full-on reconstruction with Afghanistan, Iraq, and Sudan. We remember the propaganda afterward that obscured, distorted, and defeated the truth.

When I see the cherry trees in Sakura Park, I remember all this. What do you remember?

Last cherry blossoms
the tentative steps
of old women

Cherry trees live for about sixty years in public parks, so the trees in Central Park were all replacements of the originals. A couple of centenarians survived north of East 90th Street before they succumbed to disease. The Conservancy vice-president for operations once called them "big old cranky trees." How different a sentiment from the delicacy expressed by the haiku.

Lit by the sun
the dogwood flicks
its white ash

Grandma Suzanne smoked Pall Malls and "traveled the smoke further," as the cigarette makers advertised. Grandma Nancy smoked Winstons, made by R. J. Reynolds, which sold its non-US operations to Japan Tobacco. Grandpa Larry rolled his own reefers. I imagine Grandpa Tom smoked cubeb. My parents, John and Alice, did not light up. They belonged to that generation of Americans who obeyed the surgeon general's health warnings. In any case, Alice could not abide the smoke; John, the smell. I smoke four packs of Camels a day.

The dogwood smokes dogwood.

It's too hard in spring
to study seriously
the curriculum of trees

It is madness to drop out of your studies to join a buddy on a road trip across the country, but love is a kind of madness. I met Damian Strange at Stanford's Green Library, not our usual stacks, for I was typically catalogued in the East Asia Library, and Damian, a premed student, in Lane. Yet Green was appropriate for a great number of reasons. The social sciences were the common ground on which we met. Not the mathematical abstractions of economics, nor the dusty minutia of jurisprudence, but the heaving and heady forces of political theory. Coming from a household of artists, I was looking to toughen my love of beauty with the power of judgment. Damian, descended from a distinguishable line of surgeons and hospital administrators, was seeking to soften the judgment of power with the beauty of love.

Then followed days, weeks, months of reading and debate, with the river of undergraduate fervor running through it. Damian deployed his Hobbes to dismiss my Hayek. My Sartre was marshaled against his Schmitt. When Damian got too strong, I fell back on my race and gender theorists to ambush him as he came around the corner of an argument. He wrestled me to the floor of his dorm room when my tongue got too bayonet-sharp for his liking. By the time the dust settled, and the fog cleared, we discovered we had exchanged places: he was in the jungle with Frantz Fanon, and I in the senior common room with Richard Rorty.

Our political action was not limited to our books. We engaged in campus protests, citywide marches, and cafeteria sit-ins. In 2021 and 2022, there was plenty to get angry about, what with the start of Drumpf's second term. Throughout the clamor of campaigning, Damian fell in and out of love with a succession of raven-haired women, installing first one and then another in the Oval Office of his heart. Recognizing the healthy instincts of a heterosexual male, I played the part of his chief of staff. When he grew tired of all the

political "interventions" and romantic "liaisons" and proposed a road trip, I hopped into his Toyota Yaris, and we ended up in New York City.

Then followed a languorous mood, so charmingly evoked by the haiku, when freed from political agitation and intellectual furor, we roamed the city's streets, lolled in the parks, and ate at literal holes-in-the-wall. The knowledge that we had quit school, an action more real than any protest against the killing of yet another black kid, whetted our appetite for life. In *Pirkei Avot* (*Ethics of the Fathers*), Rabbi Yaakov admonishes, "Were one to be walking on the road while studying and then stop his studies to say, 'How beautiful is this tree!' and 'How nice is this field!' such a person would be considered by the Torah to have sinned against his soul." We were guilty, joyously guilty, of taking a time-out.

The mood was not to last long. It ended abruptly when Damian met Ada Chen, the tar-haired Taiwanese.

Thumbs up
for the spring moon
undamaged headlight

You have not seen the moon until you have seen it in Yosemite Valley, bulging like a cantaloupe over Cathedral Rocks and mystical as a bridegroom above Bridalveil Fall. Sitting side by side, looking through the dirty windshield of Damian's Yaris, I was at the perigee of my orbit around him, but as for covering his sensitive wound of a mouth with my dry, scraped lint, I might as well be at the apogee.

Japanese poets beckon to the distant moon to draw it closer the way they bring some famous landscape indoors as their dry garden. Issa offers his moon to the children playing outdoors:

> Hey, you kids!
> Which one of yours is it,
> This red moon?

> (trans. Lee O-young)

Ryōkan Taigu (1758–1831) may lose everything in his house, but he still has his moon:

> A thief—
> At least he left behind
> The moon at my window

> (trans. Lee O-young)

Conversely, Korean poets do not bring the moon into their homes. According to the Korean writer Lee O-young, they prefer to appreciate it from afar.

Does grass sweat
when it's cut in the spring?
the smell says yes

The haiku is at once visceral in its sensory appeal and multivalent in its literary references. The foremost allusion is to Bashō's famous haiku, collected in his *The Narrow Road to the Deep North*, here translated by Hiroaki Sato in the one-line format he champions:

Summer grass: where warriors used to dream.

Bashō wrote the haiku in Hiraizumi, where the capital of the Northern Fujiwara once stood. When Bashō arrived, nothing was left of its glory, except summer grass.

Commentators have speculated that he might have been thinking of his favorite hero Minamoto no Yoshitsune, a brilliant general in the late Heian and early Kamakura period. His military victories helped his half-brother bring the whole of Japan under his control. Yoshitsune was betrayed by the last Fujiwara lord and forced to commit seppuku.

Different stories circulated about his end, however. In one story, he was said to have escaped further north to Hokkaido. In another story, he sailed past Hokkaido to reach continental Asia and became Genghis Khan of the steppes. A third story, hardly less fabulous, had him sailing south, preceding the Sumatran prince Sang Nila Utama in discovering the island of Singapura. (Ah, ha! pounces the Singaporean school of criticism, ignoring the fact that it is just one story among many.)

Bashō's haiku, like ours, recalls the faint fragrance of forgetting-grass (*wasuregusa*) and longing-grass (*shinobugusa*) employed widely in Heian-period poetry when reminiscing about happier times or lamenting the cruelty of a lover. It was believed that planting the forgetting-grass would help one forget one's lover.

The Tales of Ise, which recounts the amorous adventures of the legendary lover Ariwara no Narihira, refers to both kinds of grass in episode 100. Both are not actually grasses, although they are called so. Forgetting-grass is the day lily and longing-grass is a kind of fern. Another botanical confusion.

Our haiku is also an obvious allusion to *Leaves of Grass* by Walt Whitman. In section 6 of "Song of Myself," a child asks, *"What is the grass?"* and Walt answers, "The beautiful uncut hair of graves." The dead still send green signs of their life through the ground. The "flag" of Whitman's American optimism, the "hopeful green stuff" corresponds to the haiku's sweaty yes.

Many commentators have pointed out the allusion in our haiku to the Gospel of Matthew, chapter 6, verses 28–30, where Jesus said: "And why take ye thought for raiment? Consider the lilies of the field, how they grow; they toil not, neither do they spin: And yet I say unto you, That even Solomon in all his glory was not arrayed like one of these. Wherefore, if God so clothe the grass of the field, which to day is, and to morrow is cast into the oven, *shall he* not much more *clothe* you, O ye of little faith?"

Bill Clintwood follows Monica Lowstutter in comparing the plural "they" in the Bible verses to the singular "it" in the haiku. Whereas Jesus emphasizes God's care for the many, our poet stresses our common human condition.

I have discovered a further link in the New Testament commentary of the German Protestant divine Heinrich August Wilhelm Meyer (1800–1873). In his note to Jesus's sermon, Meyer informs us that lilies "grow wild in the East, without cultivation by human hands." When Jesus referred to the grass of the field, he was thinking of "the *genus* under which the lilies (which grow among the grass) are

included, and that intentionally with a view to point them out as *insignificant.*" In this reading, lilies are not different from grass, but are grass. Our haikuist, who gave himself the sobriquet of "an insignificant poet," is only as insignificant as any other poet.

Despite the Biblical allusions, the question-and-answer format of the haiku does not lend the poem the character of a catechism. Rather, it conveys an air of intimacy, more akin to the poems by Bashō and Whitman. Or to the poem "Under the Linden" by that most gifted of German *Minnesingers* Walther von der Vogelweide (c. 1170–1230):

> Under the linden
> on the heath,
> Where my sweetheart sat with me,
> There you can find
> Broken, both
> Colorful flowers and grass.
> In the nearby woods, with ringing sound
> Tandaradei!
> So sweetly sang the nightingale.

"Tandaradei" is usually glossed as onomatopoeic imitation of nightingale song. Japanese philosopher-priest Dōgen Zenji, the founder of the Sōtō school of Zen, provides a further gloss: "Grass, flowers, the landscape itself, have brought some people into the Buddha Way. Merely grasping earth or sand has caused others to receive and preserve the Buddha-mind Seal. This means that the greatest words are the ones whose abundant meanings overflow from every existing thing."

"Tandaradei," like the haiku's yes, is one of those words with overflowing meanings. Unlike the semantic fascist Konrad Boguslawski, we must refrain from pinning down just one. English critic William

Empson was particularly perceptive about the ways that a word is conservatively limited to a particular meaning. In his inimitably ironic manner, he described "the conservative attitude to ambiguity" as wise. It allows a variety of meanings to be shown in a note, but it encourages us to think that Shakespeare can only have meant one thing. The different meanings are to be weighed "according to their probabilities." The talk of "probabilities" is Empson the mathematician's joke. The weighing of literary probabilities can receive no firm grounding anywhere. To make a stand on a piece of ground is already to prejudge the range of possibilities, prefigured as close to or far off from the mark, familiar or foreign. We accept such weightings as natural only if we abide by what Empson called mockingly "a decent reserve." The English professor who taught for years in Japan and China, and for many summers in Kenyon College in Ohio, would question the parochialism of such reserve, a word whose cognate "reservation" spelled disaster for Native Americans. Should we sweat when the meanings of a word are cut to merely one? The smell of the prairies says yes.

Silken orchids
cut from the spring rain
by bandage scissors

A psychedelic fancy or its parody? The Beatles or Zappa? I put my shekels on Zappa. In the 1968 album *We're Only in It for the Money*, Zappa asks the punk where he is going with the flower in his hand. The Flower Punk is going to the love-in to sit and play his bongos before he makes a record of his music and sells it for lots of money, enough to go into real estate.

My granduncle Franklin Kaufman would have gone into real estate, just like his father, had he survived his fling with the flower punks. He was in it not for the money—he had plenty—but for the feeling of living in the stream of things. Conceived in the darkest days of World War II, he was named in honor of the sitting president, who declared war on the Krauts and the Japs. Ten years younger than Grandma Suzanne, he was the pet of the family. After going to the most prestigious private schools in Upper Manhattan, he scandalized his family, including his doting sister, by decamping to San Francisco at the height of the rock-and-roll fever. The anti-establishment antics of the flower children are laughable. On his first day in Haight-Ashbury, Granduncle Franklin died, absurdly, of an overdose of barbiturates sold to him as LSD.

His mourning sister would name her son Franklin after her brother, a name to which her husband would assent, for the president's socialism, if not for his reception of European Jewry. My uncle Franklin Mayer would kill himself fighting in Iraq for the American empire. His tank stopped by a mine outside Baghdad, he and his crew were cut down by Iraqi machine guns acquired years earlier with the help of the CIA. The American-led coalition would overthrow Saddam Hussein and unleash civil war in the country.

Why did Franklin Mayer join the army? What moved him to thrust his unimproved mettle into the fray? There is absolutely no tradition of military service in the family. Was another family history at work?

In his own desperate self-fashioning, was he trying to rewrite his father's Jewish tragedy or his uncle's American comedy? In any case, there was no ram in a bush to be found for him.

Late spring
outside reverse fold
of early fall

In *Smaller Is Better: Japan's Mastery of the Miniature*, Lee O-young makes the case for the folded fan as a Japanese invention. The Chinese and the Egyptians had the flat fans first, made from the tail feathers of a quail, according to Chinese legend. When the flat fan arrived in Japan, it was folded by the Japanese propensity to make things smaller and thus easier to carry around. In this haiku, two seasons are folded into one another, in a figure borrowed from another distinctively Japanese art, which Lee does not examine—the art of origami.

An old man sleepy
in his foldable wheelchair—
bottom of the page

Konrad Boguslawski's bogus claim that the senior citizen in the haiku is none other than the media mogul R----- M------ has been taken up by many commentators. The main basis of the claim is the reference in the word "page" to M------'s newspaper empire.

The Squat Tsar and his followers disagree over whether the third line of the haiku—"bottom of the page"—conveys a loss of power and prominence. His followers argue that the old man has fallen (asleep) from the headline to the bottom line, and so the two parts of the haiku are consonant with each other. Boguslawski insists that the two parts form a contrast instead. The bottom of the page is where you insert your signature, the highly individualized sign of one's personal authority.

Both sides are wrong. The old man is not R----- M------. Boguslawski and his party are not familiar with the genre of Japanese poems known as *mono no na no uta*, literally, "name of something poem." This kind of poem has a naming word hidden in it. We can see immediately that the haiku cannot spell out R----- M------ because it lacks any "u." I have emboldened the scattered letters that spell out the hidden name. Our haiku (in the English) is an example of *mono no na no uta*, and it hides the name of Woody Allen.

The prolific writer would have appreciated the visual and verbal puns in the folding over of both man and wheelchair, and the metaphysical conceit of "bottom of the page" for the end of life. Life is a struggle to obtain top billing, and then a precipitous fall from it, as the stand-up comedian understood.

In Allen's first directorial effort, *What's Up, Tiger Lily?* (1966), he redubbed the Japanese B movie *Key of Keys* into English, changing the spy thriller into a search for a secret egg salad recipe. The recipe is

needed to bring a country into existence, as the Grand Exalted High Majah of Raspur explains to international spy Phil Moscowitz.

Some sleuthing turns up that the original Phil Moscowitz character in *Key of Keys* was named Jiro Kitami and was played by the Japanese actor Tatsuya Mihashi. In *What's Up, Tiger Lily?*, Phil Moscowitz, who always has sex on his mind, has the body of Tatsuya Mihashi and the voice of Woody Allen. On first viewing the film, one is impressed by how completely the voice dominates the body, making it say what the voice wishes to say and making it mean what the voice wishes to mean. Subsequent viewings show, however, that the voice is actually in service of the body.

This is nowhere so clear in the movie as in its best gag, when our hero warns the casino croupier, "Don't tell me what to do, or I'll have my mustache eat your beard." The gag would have been impossible if our hero had not worn a sharp mustache and the croupier a wispy chin. The translation of our haiku into English has retained the "voice," or name, of Woody Allen but appears to have lost the "body" of the original referent. We may never find out who was hidden by our haikuist in his *mono no na no uta*. I have thought long and hard about it, but there is no Japanese filmmaker quite like Woody. However, the loss is more apparent than real, since "Woody Allen" serves a body that is more present by being absent. The original exists by being missing, or to be more accurate, by being missed. This is a point well understood by true artists. By arguing for R----- M------, the owner of bodies, media, and things, Boguslawski misses the point.

Fallen clumps
of shriveled blossoms
Nabokov's brown wigs

The reference is to "the brown wigs of tragic old women who had just been gassed," which comes from the novel *Lolita*, written in the USA by Russian author-in-exile Vladimir Nabokov. The novelist, as Nabokov saw, is a master of disguises. In *Pale Fire*, the author's stand-in Charles Kinbote, a lunatic who fancies himself a king exiled from the imaginary country of Zembla, conjures up a fictional assassin called Gradus. The novel, posing as a long poem in four cantos, with a running commentary by Kinbote, derives whatever narrative momentum it possesses from the gradual closing in of assassin on prey.

On his way to New Wey, Gradus stops in New York City and drops in on its famous park.

> He had never visited New York City before; but as many near-cretins, he was above novelty. On the previous night he had counted the mounting rows of lighted windows in several skyscrapers, and now, after checking the height of a few more buildings, he felt that he knew all there was to know. He had a brimming cup and half a saucerful of coffee at a crowded and wet counter and spent the rest of the smoke-blue morning moving from bench to bench and from paper to paper in the westside alleys of Central Park.

Here lies the fatal weakness of the novel as an art form. It has to keep moving, or else it is nothing. Its antithesis is not the poem, which can harbor the fugitive narrative, but the haiku.

Still, Nabokov has this exactly right: the love-hate relationship the commentator has with his poet. Charles Kinbote fed his poet stories of his mythical country of Zembla in the hope that the poet would bring his lost country to life and so restore it to him. When Kinbote discovered that the poem "Pale Fire" is not about Zembla but about

the tragic death of the poet's twenty-four-year-old daughter, another clump of shriveled blossoms, he proceeded to speak of Zembla in his commentary, using as an excuse any serendipitous word in the text.

A dropped napkin
dabs at the corner
of the field

It is impossible to speak of the history of the Japanese haiku in America and not speak of the history of the Japanese people in America. And it is impossible to speak of the history of the Japanese people in America and not speak of the history of their incarceration by their own government in concentration camps during World War II.

According to then–secretary of war Henry Stimson, "The very fact that no sabotage has taken place to date is a disturbing and confirming indication that such action will be taken." This surreal haiku tells of the disorienting experience of having one's land seized and swallowed illegally on such a basis as Stimson's words articulate.

The *Issei*, or first-generation Japanese immigrants, were forbidden by law to own land, and so they went around the prohibition by buying land in the name of their America-born offspring. My own great-grandfather's parents bought one hundred acres of land near Manzanar, California, in the name of their son, Paul Fujimoto. As Michi Weglyn told it in her groundbreaking report *Years of Infamy: The Untold Story of America's Concentration Camps* (1976), the Issei bought up land nobody wanted—barren deserts, swamplands, and lands dangerously close to high-tension wires, dams, and railroad tracks—and turned them into lush-growing fields. Fierce economic competition caused West Coast groups to cry foul and push for the evacuation of the Japanese from their homes, so that they could take over the now-lucrative real estate.

We must call attention to a mistake made by Rey Morse. In their commentary on this haiku, they drew attention to Rube Goldberg's 1931 cartoon *Professor Butts and the Self-Operating Napkin*. Born in San Francisco in 1883, of Jewish parents, Rube Goldberg moved to New York City, where he created Professor Lucifer Gorgonzola Butts, the mad inventor of comically complicated machines.

The Self-Operating Napkin is one such joke: Butts lifts his soup spoon, which pulls a string attached to a lever, which activates a ladle to toss a slice of bread to a bird, which flies off one end of a seesaw, which topples a tiny bowl of water into a small bucket, which pulls down one end of a balancing beam, which releases at the other end the top of a lighter, which sets on fire a rocket, which takes off and cuts with a sickle another string, which snaps and releases a clock's pendulum, which swings and carries the napkin, which wipes Butt's mouth. According to Morse, the haiku adds to the comedy by dropping the napkin, after the complicated maneuvers of the Rube Goldberg machine.

Morse's interpretation would turn the haiku into a self-ironizing joke. My interpretation reads the haiku instead as a moment of high tragedy. I submit that the two interpretations are mutually exclusive, like the Wittgensteinian rabbit/duck, or the name of Wittgenstein's paternal grandfather, Moses Meier, who adopted Wittgenstein as his surname in obedience to a Napoleonic decree. As the grandson of old Meier/Wittgenstein argued, perception is an act of interpretation, organized by our theories, experience, and language—that is, our past.

Re: Morse's interpretation, it does have this going for it—they further compare the art of commentary to a Rube Goldberg machine. The Jew in me appreciates the joke. Which reminds me of another commentary-related jest, this one from the field of Classics. "Where do you go to find a lost hankie?" an Italian professor asked his students. When they looked bemused, he replied, "In Fraenkel's *Agamemnon*. It's got everything."

What's holding up
the clouds
in the treeless sky?

Ikkyū (1394–1481) styled himself Errant Cloud, or Kyoun. His funny idiosyncrasies are captured in folktales, which my mother Alice read to me in awkward English translations, illustrated with beautiful woodblock prints, at bedtime. Errant Cloud lives on as "Little Ikkyū" in the popular culture of modern Japan.

In such a childlike spirit, our haiku alludes to one of his poems, which in turn refers to the moment on Vulture Peak when the Buddha held up a flower, and his disciple Mahākāśyapa showed his understanding by giving a slight smile.

> Holding up the Flower, Slight Smile
> From the assembly on Vulture Peak to the here and now;
> From the cave in Cockleg Mountain to the eons yet to come;
> A poisoned person certainly knows poison's use.
> In India and in this land: the same tricky fox.
>
> (trans. Ichikawa Hakugen)

Ikkyū's poem is remarkable in suggesting that this original moment for Zen Buddhism did not just take place long ago on Vulture Peak, in the state of Bihar, India, but in Ikkyū's Lake Biwa, in our here and now. We do not have only the consequences of enlightenment, but we can own the very moment of enlightenment. Every place is, or at least can be, Vulture Peak, even Cockleg Mountain. Even New York's Central Park.

What do I have
to do with clouds
but look

This haiku has the strong strokes, bold abstraction, and playful spirit of Sesshū's ink-wash paintings. Born in 1420, in Akahama, a settlement in Bitchu Province, now part of Okayama Prefecture, Sesshū Tōyō was deeply influenced by the Chinese Song Dynasty painters. He visited China in 1468 and stayed there for close to two years. When he returned to Japan, he established a large following, subsequently known as the school of Sesshū.

Isamu Noguchi was very taken by Sesshū's famous "Four Seasons" scroll when he visited Japan after World War II. His Japanese companion and fellow artist Saburo Hasegawa, who showed him the scroll, recalled, "He stared at it as though punching holes in it with his gaze."

Urban anthropologist C. T. Bee provides a more sinister take on the haiku. In his book *Drop Dead: The Drone Eye's View* (2045), he argued that the traditional "flat" perspectives that have dominated our knowledge of human societies, from cartography to surveillance footage, dilute the densities and erase the inequities that organize cities. Individual particulars are hidden from the grand view above.

Every act of looking is political. Drones were first used for targeted killing on February 4, 2002, in Paktia province, Afghanistan. In her 2009 *New Yorker* article "The Predator War," Jane Mayer described how "a Predator reportedly followed and killed three suspicious Afghans, including a tall man in robes who was thought to be bin Laden." The man and his two friends turned out to be innocent villagers collecting scrap metal, and not the terrorist leader. Pentagon spokeswoman Victoria "Torie" Clarke said at the time, "We're convinced that it was an appropriate target," and then she added, "We do not know yet exactly who it was."

The US government's targeted assassination program was renamed the Disposition Matrix, which suggested falsely that people on the kill list could be "disposed" of in any number of ways, not only by murder. The White House still observes "Terror Tuesday" every week when the POTUS gives personal approval to death without legal process. The Russians, the Chinese, the British, and even the Swiss have rapidly followed the US example, as have fifty-four other countries and counting.

Our haiku prompts us to look out, look above, for drones, now ubiquitous as clouds and acceptable as rain.

Mist over Hudson
most itself
when least

Blond hair: hair that is least like hair.

The wind is rising
I'm listening to the dark tints
of a crow etching

The haiku wrong-foots the reader every step of the way. A rising wind is, first and foremost, felt, not heard. One does not listen to colors of whatever hue, but sees them instead. Finally, the dark tints are not the coloration of a crow, but that of an etching of the bird.

There is no avoiding it. I have to speak of what I most loath to do. The wind is not just rising, but battering at my skull. Damian Strange and crow-haired Ada Chen met at Belvedere Castle, at the exact midpoint of Central Park. Like the stagey venue, the meeting was a Victorian folly. I was looking, for the umpteenth time, for a vantage point from which I could see the whole of Turtle Pond, when Damian wandered from my side into the family-friendly exhibit in the observatory tower. A display of telescopes and microscopes was posed and supposed to teach the naturalist's way of looking. More portentous of the disaster of their romance were the bird skeletons and feathers on show. By the plywood tree, under a papier-mâché red-breasted nuthatch, they walked into each other, literally. I have always suspected that Ada spotted Damian from a distance and bumped him with full lascivious intentions. Their chests met with a jolt, and then, in the confusion, Damian's hands were introduced briefly to Ada's breasts, through her "I heart Taiwan" T-shirt, but not brief enough to prevent the extension of the telescope in his shorts. After bidding me a hurried goodbye, Damian left the arbor of ardor with Ada for somewhere more private, at a wind speed that destroyed the delicate measuring instruments of the National Weather Service.

When the nun Teishin learned that Ryōkan Taigu was visiting the nearby castle town of Yoita, she hurried there to meet the famous monk and poet. Originally from a samurai family, Teishin was not slow to strike. Coquettishly, she teased the monk, "Your complexion is dark and your robe is dark, so from now on I will call you a crow." Ryōkan was supposedly so tickled by this none-too-subtle come-on that he sent her this poem:

Tomorrow
I will fly away
to who knows where,
as someone has made me
a crow.

(trans. Kazuaki Tanahashi)

In response, Teishin wrote:

Oh mountain crow,
if you are going home,
please bring along
a young crow,
even one with fragile wings.

(trans. Kazuaki Tanahashi)

Damian and Ada became inseparable. I was sometimes allowed to tag along, at which times I cleverly endeavored to get into Ada's good book (she has only one) so that she would not put a full stop to our joint outings. She largely ignored me, so sure she was of her victory. If she was crowing, so was I. I was feeding on the carrion of my friendship with Damian. He had found his love and I had nothing.

Behind the blinds
ruled like foolscap
a crow calls

The foolscap may lead one to interpret the crow as a kind of muse. A scavenger muse.

John Richard Hersey was a writer who hearkened to the crow. I cannot prove that our haikuist read Hersey, but their spiritual affinities are remarkable. Credited for helping to create New Journalism, which deployed fictional techniques for nonfiction reportage, John Hersey wrote the 1946 bestseller *Hiroshima*. In the story, which first ran as an article in the *New Yorker*, Hersey traced the effects of the bomb on six individuals written up like characters.

Four years later, in 1950, Hersey published the first American novel of the Holocaust, *The Wall*, based in part on his visits as a war correspondent to newly liberated Nazi concentration camps. He presented the work as a rediscovered journal by a fictional historian and resident of the Warsaw Ghetto Noach Levinson, who is recording the story of forty ghetto survivors of Nazi persecution. The fictional diary won the National Jewish Book Award.

Then, in 1988, his fifteen-thousand-word text, which accompanies photographs of the Manzanar concentration camp by Ansel Adams, was published as "A Mistake of Terrifically Horrible Proportions." In reviewing the book, British literary biographer Jeremy Treglown praised Hersey for his ability to convey the grit of lived experience. He also praised Hersey for not conflating the events and the camps in Europe and America. They are obviously not the same, not even remotely symmetrical, but they share the similar theme of undeserved mass suffering caused solely, soully, by one's race.

John Hersey costumed himself in the feathers of the crow, upstart and otherwise, in an even more spectacular fashion. He was guilty of plagiarism. For his *New Yorker* essay about James Agee, he took complete paragraphs from the Agee biography by Laurence Bergreen.

Even more damaging, half of his book *Men on Bataan* came from work filed for *Time* by Melville Jacoby and his wife, Annalee Whitmore Fadiman.

There came a time, I suppose, when a writer felt that his work was so important to the world that a petty sin like plagiarism should not stand in the way. He owned a double mind about himself. He was at once important and unimportant. He was important because of the work *to be done*. He was unimportant because of *the work* to be done. Like our haikuist, he listened to the cawing coming from behind the blinds.

An owl's calling
wakes up a late spring morning
to wit, who who who

Sounding the base word "who" of Ginsberg's "Howl," the haiku outright challenges the reader to find out who wrote it. Many readers have made it their vocation, or "calling," to prove the identity of the author (see my Preface). And like Cyril Graham in the story "The Portrait of W. H." by Oscar Wilde, a select few committed a forgery—who who who—in order to prove their theory.

There was A. Gizō, the Asian American studies professor at Ursuline College, founded by the Ursuline Sisters of Cleveland in 1871. A. Gizō claimed that the insignificant poet was Yone Noguchi (1875–1947), the father of the sculptor Isamu Noguchi. To prove her wild conjecture, she commissioned an obscure Japanese American artist to create a scroll painting of the forsythia by the reservoir. To clinch her point, she forged a poem supposedly by Yone Noguchi by reverse-translating one of our poet's haiku into Japanese:

> Going incognito
> the forsythia drops
> its medals

> *Inpei ni naru rengyou kara kin ga ochiru*

The Japanese haiku was added to the painting by a man familiar with Yone Noguchi's style of calligraphy and signed off with the name of the poet.

The most intriguing hoax was perpetrated by the Afrikaans writer Vals Crux. It was of the utmost delicacy. He suggested that the insignificant poet was none other than the composer John Cage, my father's eidolon. [Transcriber's note: SFM's spelling was remarkably good, but here he misspelled "eidolon" as "edolon."] Other commentators following Crux's suggestion tried to find connections between

Cage's work and our poet's haiku, alighting most frequently on *Cheap Imitation*.

The 1969 composition, a solo piano work, was created using the *I Ching* and the rhythmic structure of *Socrate* by Erik Satie. Cage was transcribing the Satie work for a choreographic piece by Merce Cunningham. Refused permission by Satie's publisher to perform *Socrate*, Cage had to keep the rhythmic structure, upon which the choreography was based, but changed the pitches by consulting the *I Ching*. The work was clearly a departure from Cage's ideas on the impersonality of art. He would later explain that departure as the result of his passion for Satie: "In the rest of my work, I'm in harmony with myself. . . . But *Cheap Imitation* clearly takes me away from all that. So if my ideas sink into confusion, I owe that confusion to love." Unlike his imitators and followers, Vals Crux refused to provide any proof for his theory and claimed to have thereby proven it.

A researcher into electronic music and artificial intelligence, Chip "Ransom" Ware wrote a computer program to generate haiku. He then published a book in which some poems were written by the machine and others were written by human beings, leaving the reader to agonize over which was which. He, too, chimed in on the identity of our haikuist and suggested that he or she was an it, a computer program like his, but more primitive.

Gizō's hoax was discovered when an art historian and lover of these haiku found four paintings of forsythia, very small, all measuring six-by-six inches, in an antique shop in Hudson, New York, named after the river that the explorer Henry Hudson thought would lead him to Cathay. He—the art historian, not the sea explorer—recognized the style as the one in the supposed Yone Noguchi scroll and, after a dogged investigation too tedious to describe in full here, found the obscure Japanese American artist who identified the scroll as his work

when the art historian showed him a photograph of it on his phone. At least, that is the story given out. The obscure Japanese American artist is neither obscure, nor Japanese American, nor a he. I will now reveal her identity in these pages. She is none other than my dear artist mother, the lover of Bashō, Buson, and Issa in translation, Alice Mayer.

In the impaired ear
of the tall dark-haired boy
a small seashell

Both East Asian and Jewish mysticism represent the divine element in human beings as a kind of soul-breath. In the *Zhuangzi*, Sir Motley of Southurb explains to Sir Wanderer of Countenance Complete the divine origins of this breath:

> The Great Clod emits a vital breath called the wind. If it doesn't blow, nothing happens. Once it starts to blow, however, myriad hollows begin to howl. Have you not heard its moaning?

(trans. Victor H. Mair)

Similarly, the author of the Zohar insists that the *neshamah* (soul-breath) is "unknowable except through the limbs of the body, subordinates of *neshamah* who carry out what she designs." He goes further. Quoting *Keter Malkbut* by Solomon ibn Gabirol, the author of the Zohar describes the Blessed Holy One as "*Neshamah* of *neshamah*" and explains that the Blessed Holy One is known through the gates, or openings, in the world and the body.

Hearing aids disappeared in 2024 with the advance of cochlear implants. Our haikuist observed a deaf child with a hearing aid in his ear and saw not an impairment in the gate of the body but an enhancement that brought the sound of the ocean to him. Nevertheless, the haiku evokes the same sadness of loss as that part of the *Heike monogatari* in which a flute is found on the body of the young warrior Atsumori killed by the sea, first pointed out by Helen Snow. Or the discovery of a slim volume of haiku in the coat pocket of a dead political activist not yet twenty-five years old.

Over the scaffold
by the side of the girls' school
a big butterfly net

The unity of this haiku is as powerful and subtle as the Prussian blue that unites Mount Fuji, the waves, and the fishermen returning home with their catch in the great woodblock print *Under the Wave off Kanagawa* by Katsushika Hokusai. The pigment, then newly available from China to Japanese artists, stands for the early light of morning. As the series *Thirty-Six Views of Mount Fuji* developed, Hokusai introduced other colors to represent the changing lights of the progressing day. When the series was published, Hokusai was seventy-one. Our haiku, too, possesses the air of having been written at an advanced age.

Summer breeze—
a pint of blueberries
from the store

The haiku has the appeal of carefree and available sensation. Arthur Arthur drew attention to the eroticism of the blueberries. Not just in the sexual innuendo of blue balls, but also in the near-homonym of *pint* and *pine*. A pint is originally a measurement of liquid. Here it suggests the juice to be drawn from the blueberries.

Or the haiku is related to the fruit farms on the West Coast that Japanese Americans had to surrender when they were incarcerated by their own government.

Take your pick.

A soap bubble
splits the sun
by the black walnut

Theses on the Philosophy of Double Suicides

1. Another elegiac haiku. The conjunction of sunlight and black branches may recall a sonnet of mourning composed by Walter Benjamin for his friend Christoph Friedrich Heinle. Better known as a cultural critic, Benjamin wrote a sequence of seventy-three sonnets in his twenties, working on them for a decade. The sonnets were unknown except to his household and closest associates. When he could no longer remain in France in 1940, Benjamin entrusted the sonnets to Georges Bataille. They were presumed lost but were rediscovered in the Bibliothèque nationale in Paris in 1981. The first sonnet of the sequence employs the standard number of rhymes in a Shakespearian sonnet, apparently in homage to the English bard's tribute to another young man.

2. Damian Strange started to write poems for Ada Chen in the spring of 2023. One a day, which he showed me before slipping it under her door. They were uniformly dreadful.

3. Benjamin met "Fritz" Heinle when they were both students at the University of Freiburg. Sitting snugly in the lap of highlands, on the edge of the Black Forest, Freiburg im Breisgau was a beautiful setting for the meeting. "Within weeks they were hiking together in the surrounding mountains and drinking together in taverns," according to the sonnets' English translator Carl Skoggard. Benjamin's sonnets and letters show that he quickly came under the intellectual and spiritual sway of his younger Rhinelander friend. He tried hard to get his friend's poems published. Together they became very active in the youth culture movement, envisioning the regeneration of German society by fully autonomous youths.

4. Ada initiated Damian into the volatile politics of Taiwanese independence. He came under the sway of long black hair, usually pinned up in a teased chignon. When Ada cut off fistfuls of her hair during a ridiculous demonstration outside the US Congress, Damian kissed the stippled scalp and kicked the cladded shins of the riot police who were bundling the do-or-die-hards, the International Vanguard, into the police van.

5. When the war came, most young men of Benjamin's age rushed to enlist, but Fritz Heinle decided otherwise. Despairing of Germany, he and his lover Rika Seligson committed suicide by gassing themselves. Who was Rika Seligson? She died with Heinle as she lived with him. Skoggard thinks that she cowrote the poems that we now consider Heinle's. The method of suicide—death by asphyxiation—says as much. They stopped singing together.

6. Taiwan declared independence, China invaded, and Uncle Sam stood aside, twiddling his treacherous thumbs. Ada and Damian were distraught. Chinese planes strafed Taipei with impunity, protected by Chinese stealth technology. Chinese tanks strolled into the capital twenty-four hours after the start of the invasion. Damian and Ada decided to kill themselves. The tar-haired beauty bought Diamond Crystal Water Softener from the Ace Hardware online store. Damian the ex-medical student injected the potassium chloride into her and then into himself. She refused to take Valium beforehand to dull the induced heart attack. Her death would sacralize the fight for Taiwan.

7. The seventh sonnet of Benjamin's sequence begins with a memory of the hikes he took with Heinle in the Black Forest.

How should I joy in this day's gleamings
Comest thou with me not into the woods

Where through black branches sunlight flashes
Which thy piercing gaze once could renew

8. Have I told you yet that Ada Chen has, had, beautiful handwriting? She grew up in Taiwan where they still taught handwriting, not just "keyboard skills." She had overly big hands, which she hid behind her or behind your back when she hugged you instead of shaking hands. But those ungainly instruments obtained the most graceful writing. I once came upon a grocery list in her hand and kept it. It is lost now, but I can still remember what she wanted Damian to get from the stores:

> blueberries (1 box, 2 if discount)
> milk (full cream)
> spaghetti (whole wheat)
> chicken (cheapest you can find)
> fresh pesto
> garlic
> shiitake (mushrooms)
> ladies' fingers (aka okra)

9. Skoggard in his commentary on Benjamin's sonnet points out that "a peculiar erotic intimacy results when the friend's *physical* finger etches signs on (or in) the *mind* of the poet," both emphases his.

10. A black walnut tree used to stand near the 85th Street exit of Central Park. Just before the exit, a young black man could often be seen, when the weather was right, making giant soap bubbles with a long piece of string. A bubble would float toward the black walnut and explode upon contact but not before refracting the sunlight into its constituent characters. Before Ada came into the picture, Damian and I would sit on the park bench and watch

the open-air soap opera. After she burst into his life, I would sit by myself on that park bench. Without the need for a string, my mind conjured up magical images of their sexual bliss, she riding him with her dark hair washing down her breasts and back, he lying back into a river of joy, the look on his face recognizable from that which he showed me when he pointed out the moon in Yosemite. Ada and Damian. Damian and Ada. They found themselves wholly in one another, their names an anagram of the other's. Ada's Chinese name was Min.

The moon tonight
tosses its horns
at the trumpet's lion

Does this haiku fulfill the criterion set out by Huineng (638–713), the Sixth Zen Ancestor? According to Huineng, haiku is like a finger pointing at the moon. Once you've seen it, you no longer need the finger. Huineng was illiterate, but the learned medieval Jewish scholar Maimonides (1135–1204) held a similar opinion. In discussing the Torah, a man's words should be few but full of meaning, he thought.

In the green pond
sunning turtles point the way
to Mecca

The Turtle Pond under Belvedere Castle in Central Park was redesigned in 1997 so that no single vantage point can reveal the true extent of the pond. In this aspect, it resembles the famous Zen garden of Ryōan-ji. The stones in the dry garden are placed in such a manner that the entire composition cannot be grasped at once. At any human vantage point, one can only see fourteen of the fifteen stones.

Looking at the turtles sunning themselves on rocks, our haikuist was reminded of the green color of Islam and so extended the unknowability of the pond to Mecca, where the Kaaba, the ancient central building of the Great Mosque, holds the Black Stone in its eastern corner. The sacred Stone supposedly fell from heaven to show Adam and Eve where to build a temple. It is not one stone but many, held together by cement and a silver frame.

Some would call the stones fragments, but since the Stone iself is a fragment of a larger stone, and the larger stone a fragment of an even larger stone, and so on, we can safely call the sacred relic the Black Stones instead. In the same way, one may think of a haiku as a fragment and a whole.

Konrad Boguslawski points to this haiku as another example of the collection's impurities. What does Islam have to do with Issa, or Mecca to do with Manhattan, he asks alliteratively. The question smacks of racial prejudice and betrays cultural ignorance. The Black Stones are held together as the Black Stone by a technique that resembles the Japanese art of *wari modoshi*, or splitting and returning.

The estate cat
is stalking the ducklings—
a gymnast flexes his six pack

The Colombian writer Ignacio Zubieta, an outstanding athlete, loved to quote Frantz Fanon on the necessity and beauty of action:

> When the colonized intellectual writing for his people uses the past he must do so with the intention of opening up the future, of spurring them into action and fostering hope. But in order to secure hope, in order to give it substance, he must take part in the action and commit himself body and soul to the national struggle. You can talk about anything you like, but when it comes to talking about that one thing in a man's life that involves opening up new horizons, enlightening your country, and standing tall alongside your own people, then muscle power is required.

The ducklings are not the six pack, as Konrad Boguslawski would have it, a reading which aligns the cat with the gymnast. The ducklings are, instead, the wretched of the earth. Stalked by the territorial cat, they require the help of the gymnast well-trained for action, Fanon's intellectual who will exert his "muscle power."

Ryhen Lovable picks up on the queer tenor of the haiku and relates it to the early liberationist rhetoric of the Gay Liberation Front. He points to the book *Deep Gossip* by Henry Abelove, which argues that the Front's rhetoric was influenced by its reading of queer writers such as James Baldwin, Elizabeth Bishop, Paul Bowles, Jane Bowles, and Frank O'Hara, who had witnessed the post–World War II decolonization movement abroad and wrote about it. As Abelove argued, "The common view of early gay liberation as an identity politics is mistaken. New York's GLF was not predicated on a commitment to a supposititiously stable or definite identity. It was rather predicated on a commitment to a worldwide struggle for decolonization and its potential human benefits."

A butterfly and I pass each other
my pearl anklet
its morning brush with death

The guards at Lod Airport (now called Ben Gurion) in Tel Aviv were looking out for Palestinian terrorists and so were surprised when three Japanese passengers removed automatic weapons from their suitcases and started shooting in the baggage claim area.

Between them, Kōzō Okamoto, Yasuyuki Yasuda, and Tsuyoshi Okudaira killed twenty-six people, including renowned protein biophysicist Aharon Katzir, and injured seventy-one others. Yasuda and Okudaira themselves died in the attack. Members of the Japanese Red Army, the terrorists were working with the Popular Front for the Liberation of Palestine—External Operations. The idea behind the joint attack was for the JRA to carry out attacks for the PFLP-EO and vice versa, in order to escape suspicion. It succeeded too well.

My mother, Alice Mayer, was born on the day of the massacre, May 30, 1972. It was yet another reason my grandmother never forgave her daughter for marrying a Japanese man. Leaving home was my mother's way of getting away from these old hatreds. It was a foolish and forlorn hope. The past is not dead, etc.

A butterfly passes our haikuist one early morning. It is probably a cabbage white, or *Pieris rapae*, a very common butterfly, usually the first to be seen flying in the spring and the last to be seen flying in the fall. How would it know that the human foot could so easily stamp the pearl anklet to smithereens?

Smell of garbage
no garbage truck in sight
the fly follows me inside

The haiku is full of the spirit of Issa, the soul of humorous self-mockery. It preys on garbage. Appealing!

Workman carrying
an attachable barrier
past a blonde

The French poet and translator Nicolas Pesquès once said, to write is to embody; to translate is to trace corporeally the same path that the first body took. The impossibility of translation is the impossibility of two bodies occupying the same space at the same time.

The German author Friedrich Schiller expressed a similar sentiment in a more dramatic key:

> The world is narrow, broad the mind—
> Thoughts dwell easily side by side
> Things collide violently in space.

Our Insignificant Japanese Poet invented a highly original image for the human body: one of those plastic road barriers that come in either white or orange. If workman and blonde cannot occupy the same space at the same time, they can yet lock barrier to barrier and make a protected space for translation.

Alice Mayer and John Fujimoto agreed with our poet.

This london plane
an uncertain time machine
couples walk by

Alice Mayer and John Fujimoto first met in the Cohen Family Studio Theater at the Cincinnati College-Conservatory of Music. She was there to watch and he was there to hear (with his eyes closed) the blond virtuoso Brad Vogel perform John Cage's *Water Walk*. Afterward they agreed that it was the closest thing to the master's own performance on the popular sixties TV show "I've Got a Secret," although Alice pointed out that Vogel lowered the wrong kind of roses into the bathtub. John was in no position to disagree, especially since he was already entranced by Alice's stutter. Wrong flow-ow-ow-ow-er. Embarrassed for her, though she displayed no evidence of embarrassment, he held back from asking for her number. He did not want the short and dark girl to think that he pitied her.

The next time they met was by the operatic operation of chance again. On a Sunday, Alice visited a new girlfriend in Amberley Village, who took her to Fuji Sushi for lunch. The restaurant had become fancy under Grandma Nancy, with track lighting and excellent reproductions of Hokusai's woodblock prints, but it was still staffed by grudging family members. This time, John did not hold back. While bringing Alice her special-order unagi roll, and thereby discovering that this Jewish lass did not keep kosher, John asked her out. Alice, somewhat to her own surprise, said yes.

John kept the budding relationship a secret from his mom, knowing Nancy's dislike for Jews, although the dislike in no way inhibited her from accepting their money. He had to tell her finally when Alice became pregnant. The young and passionate couple had been extremely careful since both were intensely ambitious artists in their own quiet way, and they knew that having a child right then would halt the momentum of their creative development and artistic careers. But one Saturday afternoon, after a long day in the editing studio, John was trying to relax in a hot bath at home when Alice, covered with blue paint in her hair and naked everywhere else, climbed in and

on top of him. I was conceived at that moment, so my parents told me, and I had John Cage to thank or to blame.

With Nancy's reluctant blessings, the wedding was planned for June. In March, Alice received news that her brother, Franklin Mayer, had died in the Iraq War. His death hung like a ghostly garland over the garden wedding. In memory of the dead soldier and in defiance of superstition, bride and groom and guests observed a silence of four minutes and thirty-three seconds. Someone—was it second cousin Yuki, who later died in the Third Gulf War?—swore he heard artillery fire in the distance.

Alice Mayer was short and dark like her father. John Fujimoto was short and dark like his mother. I inherited the looks of the uglier sides of both families. The best photo of my parents that I own is one of them in Central Park. It was early in their courtship, and they were visiting New York together for the first time. They looked brilliantly happy under the London plane near the West 86th Street entrance. They were in love and full of hope for their self-chosen professions. Through their love and their art, they would live away from their parents and outside of history, so their faces in the photo said.

The happiness was not to last. They divorced when I was eight.

Hold your breath
on a dandelion stalk
full moon

In his note on the poem by Ryōkan Taigu beginning:

> All seasons have the moon,
> and yet we admire it especially in autumn

translator Kazuaki Tanahashi glossed "transmission on Vulture Peak" in this manner:

> According to a Zen legend, in a great assembly on Vulture Peak, in the kingdom of Magadha [SFM: in northeast India], Shakyamuni Buddha said: "I have the treasury of the true dharma eye, the wondrous heart of nirvana. Now I entrust it to Mahakashyapa." The disciple received the transmission because he understood the Buddha's wordless Flower Sermon. When the Buddha held up a white flower, all the other disciples did not know what to say, but Mahakashyapa understood and smiled slightly, and so initiated a way of enlightenment within Buddhism, according to the Zen school, which concentrates on direct experience, rather than on doctrines or scriptures.

The story of the Flower Sermon appears to have been created by Chinese Chán Buddhists, and the earliest known version dates back to 1036 only. Words matter, after all. None of the versions of the story specifies what the white flower was. The point here, as I understand it, is not that the kind of flower was not important, but that the flower could have been of any kind.

It could have been the dandelion used by the ancient Chinese, Egyptians, and Greeks as both food and herb, and for that purpose carried over to North America on the Mayflower. Sure, the flower in bloom is yellow, but the seed head is white, with a ghostly beauty and wanton delicacy that our haiku underscores by its comparison to the moon.

The wind is rising
the shadow of the pine
holds its ground

Stories about heroes with great martial and magical prowess are very popular in East Asia, and this haiku shares their heroic ethos. To keep me rooted in my "culture" when I was growing up, my mother Alice plied me with picture books of these stories. I read them over and over again and dreamed about them constantly, but one hero, who happened to be Korean, rose above all to become the embodiment of righteous power. His name was Hong Gildong.

Because Gildong was born the "secondary" son of a high minister and a concubine, he was not allowed to call his father Father and his brother Brother. He was also not allowed to take the civil service examinations to give form to his obvious talents. When High Minister Hong was persuaded by a shaman that young Gildong would rise up against the emperor and so bring disaster on the family, he confined his talented son to a cottage at the bottom of the family estate.

There, Gildong entered a period of extreme isolation and arduous training, a characteristic stage of these heroic tales. He studied not only the military instruction in the *Six Teachings* and the *Three Summaries* but also the magical arts in the *Juyoek* (better known as the *I Ching* in the West) and learned to summon supernatural spirits and to control the wind and the rain. These accomplishments came in handy when he faced off with an assassin.

To confuse his attacker, Gildong changed the orientation of his cottage completely and attached "the fire trigram of the southward direction to the northward direction, the water trigram of the northward direction to the southward direction, the thunder trigram of the eastward direction to the westward direction, the lake trigram of the westward direction to the eastward direction, the heaven trigram of the northwestward direction to the southeastward direction, the wind trigram of the southeastward direction to the northwestward direction, the mountain trigram of the northeastward direction to the

southwestward direction, and the earth trigram of the southwestward direction to the northeastward direction," a description as disorienting for a reader as the magic was for the assassin. To maintain your balance and execute your mission successfully, you have to focus on the shadow of a pine.

In his useful introduction to *The Story of Hong Gildong*, the translator Minsoo Kang remarked that the hero is so embedded in Korean consciousness that instructions on how to fill in modern-day forms commonly use "Hong Gildong" to indicate where one's name should be written. Compare with the bland anonymity of John Doe. We are better off completing forms with the name of Clark Kent.

The tall blond tourist
puts her bag down by the tree
where the dog pissed

Next year, 2067, will mark the hundredth anniversary of Israel's annexation of West Bank and Gaza. Driven by religious nationalism and hunger for land, Israeli settlements now dominate the two territories, reducing the Palestinians to the barest sliver of their former homeland.

The cycle of violence continues, with the Seventh Intifada (2061–2063) the bloodiest yet, triggered by the annual Jerusalem Day march from Damascus Gate into the Muslim Quarter of the Old City. Israel has truly created Palestine, as surely as Palestine has created Israel. Neither can now exist without the other.

The Israeli poet Pseudo-Solomon was the first to apply this haiku jokingly to the struggle for Palestine, but what was intended as a joke was taken up as a life-and-death matter. The haiku has become one of the surest tests of a commentator's political allegiances. Pro-Israel commentators emphasize the comparison of Palestinians to dogs. Pro-Palestine commentators, such as Konrad Boguslawski, point out that the dog is only doing what dogs do to mark their territory, and no insult is necessarily intended. They highlight the description of Israel as "tourist" and underline the mockery of the woman in the haiku's tone.

My own view is that the haiku takes shots at both Israel and Palestine. Both are mocked for trying to take possession of what does not belong to them but to all of humanity. The land belongs to whoever wants to live there. Martin Buber was right when he warned that the Jews would oppress others if they set up a Jewish state. The Palestinians in their turn will do the same.

I must add here that both my Jewish grandparents were Zionists. One, a survivor of the Holocaust, the other, a survivor of the New York social calendar, they united in their fervent, and material,

support of a Jewish homeland. Not my mother, Alice Mayer, who could be trusted to oppose her parents in this matter, as in all matters. She came out for Palestinian self-determination, when she could be persuaded to come out of her studio at all.

In the rain
the tree trunks turn dark
a night with stars

Rainfall is compared ingeniously to sunset. A descant on descent.

Thank you, rain,
for calming down
the dust

In World War II, the Pacific Military Zone was defined as the area between the Pacific coast and an imaginary line along the Cascade Mountains in Washington and Oregon and down the spine of California. From that zone, Japanese and Japanese Americans were forcibly removed to concentration camps in remote and desolate locations.

The first camp to open was Manzanar War Relocation Center. It was nothing like the apple orchard of its Spanish name. Located at the foot of the Sierra Nevada in California, it was desert land, with blistering summers and freezing winters. The ever-present dust, blown about by Dantesque winds, was a continual problem. The mean (in both senses of the word) annual precipitation was barely five inches.

My paternal grandmother, Nancy Fujimoto, was born in that camp. Her mother told her that she cried endlessly because of the irritation of the dust. When she woke up from her naps, she was covered from head to toe in a quintessence of dust. The dust got inside too—eyes, ears, nose, also mouth, armpits, navel, genitals. Inside the space in between the toes called interspaces.

My great-grandmother Aiko said that the dust got inside your soul, too, so that you were less sure of everything than before. The feeling never left you, even after you left the camp. Your friends turned out not to be your friends. Your property turned out not to be yours. Little wonder that some older folks chose repatriation to Japan, where they also remained uncertain about their place in the world, their American sojourn a never-ending dust storm. And so you learned the truth of Dōgen's teaching: "The Great Dharma Wheel of preaching turns in every speck of dust."

Wild rosebush
a honeybee's dream
of red pavilions

Chinese scholars, keen to highlight the influence of Chinese literature on *Snow*, have elaborated on the manifold relationships between this haiku and the eighteenth-century novel *Dream of the Red Chamber*, by Cao Xueqin, considered one of China's Four Great Classical Novels and known for its huge cast of characters. Its opening couplet, which goes:

> Truth becomes fiction when the fiction's true;
> Real becomes not-real where the unreal's real.

blurs the boundary between truth and fiction, as in a dream.

These scholars, because of their nationalistic agenda, have neglected, however, a non-Chinese dimension to the haiku. Cao's novel is also known as *The Story of the Stone*, for its frame story of a heavenly Stone who enters the world to learn about human existence. The idea of a sentient Stone must bring to mind the work of Isamu Noguchi, in particular, his creation of a sculpture garden out of a rock-strewn hillside in Jerusalem, Israel, for the Broadway impresario Billy Rose.

At first Noguchi hesitated to accept the commission because of Rose's reputation for unpredictability, but as Noguchi's biographer Hayden Herrera told it, Rose refused to take no for an answer. His argument? "A man who voluntarily incarcerated himself in a War Relocation Camp could not refuse such a challenge."

Later Noguchi would explain his acceptance of the job in this way: "My going to Israel was in a way like going home and seeing people like myself who craved for some reason or other a particular spot on earth to call their own. . . . The Jew has always appealed to me as being the endless, continuously expatriated person who really did not belong anywhere. That is the way the artist feels."

Despite the rocky back-and-forth between client and artist, the Billy Rose Sculpture Garden was one of the achievements that Noguchi was proudest of. Writing about it in an article published in both the *Jerusalem Post* and *Arts and Architecture*, Noguchi suggested, "We are all Israelis who come here and walk its slopes." The garden, Noguchi felt, belonged to everyone. As he said elsewhere, Jerusalem was "an emotion shared by all of us."

The client was much more pragmatic. At the opening of the garden, which held Rose's donation of modern steel abstract works, a distinguished guest asked Rose what Israel should do with the sculptures in the event of war. Without losing a beat, he replied, "Melt them down for bullets."

The garden opened in 1965, two years before the Six-Day War.

Far from home
an Eastern feast
of soft-shelled crabs

This haiku alludes to the famous poem by Ishikawa Takuboku, here translated literally by the Korean writer Lee O-young:

> On the white sand of a beach
> Of a small island
> Of the Eastern sea,
> I am damp from crying
> And I toy with a crab.

Lee's translation reproduces the unique Japanese syntax of the original. Four nouns are connected in succession by the possessive particle *no*. The frequent resort to *no* is characteristic of the Japanese language, but not Chinese nor Korean. To illustrate how odd Japanese syntax appears to Koreans, Lee retells a joke that is popular among young Koreans. Not a knock-knock joke, but a tick-tock joke.

Question: Why does a Japanese clock, even one superbly made, always run several minutes behind a Korean clock?

Answer: Because the Korean clock goes "tick-tock, tick-tock," while the Japanese clock goes "tick-tock *no* tick-tock *no*."

When Great-grandpa Paul Fujimoto answered no-no to the government questionnaire, was he also saying of his confiscated farm, mine-mine?

Short summer night
the cops are eyeing the holes
in the donut joint

Soon-Tek Oh, or Soon-Taik Oh, or Soon-Taek Oh (oh, oh, oh, the confusions of transliteration!) was an American actor of Korean heritage who was often mistaken for Japanese because of his career playing characters of that ethnicity. From 1965 to 1993, he acted in many detective TV series as a houseboy, victim, tycoon, sensei, even a detective sidekick, but never the detective.

When Oh wrote his own script instead of following the script of others, he composed a two-act play titled *Tondemonai—Never Happen!* (1970) about the Japanese incarceration in World War II. He was Korean, not Japanese, but he wrote from his TV-imposed Japanese identity.

Literary historian Greg Robinson describes the play in the castrated style of the professional academic:

> The story takes place in the bunker-like basement of Koji Murayama, a Kibei former inmate, who is tortured by flashbacks of the horrors that his family experienced during their wartime confinement at Manzanar, his incarceration at Tule Lake, and a term in prison. Koji's traumatic experience has turned him into a cold, unfeeling individual. Through a sexual encounter with a young Chinese American man, Fred Chung, with whom he finds himself psychologically (and physically) stripped down, Koji starts to awaken from his numbness and begin feeling strong emotion.

The artistic question not tackled by Robinson is how to make the audience feel for cold, unfeeling Koji, who is always on the verge of becoming a cipher, a zero, an empty container of historical and personal traumas. The playwright cannot depend on the sexual transformation in Act Two to turn his zero into a hero. The audience would have walked out at intermission. The obscurity of

Tondemonai—Never Happen! suggests that Oh did not find a solution to the problem. He did not avoid the void.

At the 5th International Symposium on *Snow at 5 PM* held in New York City, the crime writer Ken Tanaka solved the mystery of our haiku. According to him, the donut joint is at once Hollywood, the gay closet, the war camps, and, most broadly, America. The haiku turns the all-seeing eyes of jailers into the greedy eyes of johns. The fascination of the keepers with the brothers is conveyed with dry-as-boner humor. We are all fucked as holes, hos, or ohs, in the donut joint of the System.

The Singapore school of criticism points out that Oh's play was written and performed in 1970, the year of Jee Leong Koh's birth. This is a stray coincidence of no importance whatsoever.

Hungry again
what good
are my neighbor's plums?

No good, unless you help yourself to them. Political speeches are full of examples of such thefts of plums. In 2008, without any attribution, the forty-fourth president, Barack Obama, delivered lines borrowed from a speech by Deval Patrick, the Massachusetts governor. Patrick asked rhetorically:

> "We hold these truths to be self-evident, that all men are created equal"—just words? Just words? "Ask not what your country can do for you, ask what you can do for your country." Just words? "I have a dream"—just words?"

Obama ventriloquised:

> Don't tell me words don't matter. "I have a dream"—just words? "We hold these truths to be self-evident, that all men are created equal"—just words? "We have nothing to fear but fear itself"—just words? Just speeches?

These instances of plagiarism are mostly caused by the writing of speeches by committee. As a speech is passed around and modified from one spin doctor to another, quotation marks are dropped, sources are deleted, ignorance is compounded. But all writing is, in a very deep sense, done by committee. We are plagiarizing the past all the time, with hardly a note to ask for forgiveness for taking the plum, so cold and sweet.

Obama took the plum job from Hillary Diane Rodham Clinton in 2009. At his presidential inauguration, all of us at Seven Hills School were marched into the assembly hall, and we watched the inauguration on the half-story-height projector screen. A knowing first-grader then, I looked around the hall and saw my teachers crying like babies. Many of them had marched on Washington in 1963. The air in the hall was so thick with emotion that you could slice it. Then came the

unspeakable disillusionment with his presidency when the Nobel Peace Prize winner slaughtered innocent civilians in Afghanistan with drones. There is no reason to believe that Clinton would have been any different.

Under the sky
and its September glint
an empty pedestal

Near to our poet's daily walk was the equestrian monument of Władysław II Jagiełło, crossing two swords over his head while gazing in triumph at Belvedere Castle. By marrying the Queen of Poland in 1386, Jagiełło united Lithuania and Poland, and by defeating the Teutonic Knights at the Battle of Grunwald in 1410, he established the Polish–Lithuanian alliance as a powerful force in Europe. Here was the beginning of Poland's golden age, cut from the flow of time by the swords.

Little wonder then that his imposing statue confronted visitors to the Polish pavilion at the 1939–40 New York World's Fair of Flushing Meadows, Queens. (Not the 1964 World's Fair, as Konrad Boguslawski mistakenly has it, where IBM showed off its machine translation.) The statue of the King was inspired by a similar memorial in the middle of Warsaw, erected by the Polish pianist and ardent nationalist Ignacy Jan Paderewski, a great friend of my great-grandfather Joseph "Klezmer" Mayer. When the victorious allies of World War I called for the "rigid protection" of minorities in Poland, in Woodrow Wilson's words, Paderewski warned them against creating a "Jewish problem" by protecting some minorities and not others. His warning was not heeded and Poland was forced to sign the Little Treaty of Versailles. Fast forward twenty-one years: the statue went up at the World's Fair, but this time, instead of keeping his arms by his side, he raised them victoriously in the air.

Then the Germans invaded Poland, historic payback for Grunwald, with devastating consequences for Polish Jews. After occupying Warsaw, the Germans melted down the original statue, arms still stuck to his sides, into bullets. The one stranded in the States was finally moved to Central Park in 1945. There, he waved his swords over the Turtle Pond and rallied to him Polish dancers, picnickers, and pigeons.

Konrad Boguslawski argues that the statue in the haiku has not been felled by time but has been taken down for restoration. He shows that King Jagiełło was removed by park authorities for restoration work in 1984, 2016, and, most recently, 2045, for the hundredth anniversary of its installation in Central Park. Seen in this light, the haiku is to be read not as a warning of divine punishment for hubris but as a paean to the heroic effort to ameliorate seasonal disrepairs.

His argument is an ingenious effort to conceal the revolutionary potential in the haiku. It is clear that the statue fell to the glinting sword of time. It is of a piece with "Ozymandias" by the English atheist Percy Bysshe Shelley. Our Oxford-trained translator might have had the Romantic poem in mind when he echoed the word "pedestal." The pleasure gardens of the sneering King are always in danger of turning into lone and level sands.

Crickets chirping:
illuminated numbers
on a digital clock

On December 7, 1941, at 7:48 a.m. Hawaiian Time, the first Japanese bombs fell on Pearl Harbor, and the news was carried by millions of radios into millions of American homes. Like stridulating crickets, patriotic Americans chirped stridently in the days ahead. If social media had been around then, Facebook and its affiliates would have been commandeered by battalions of armchair warriors.

Hearing the news of the bombing, Herman Fine in Seattle, Washington, thought of his Japanese neighbors. As John Okada records, or invents, in the preface to his novel *No-No Boy*:

> A truck and a keen sense of horse-trading had provided a good living for Herman Fine. He bought from and sold primarily to Japanese hotel-keepers and grocers. No transaction was made without considerable haggling and clever maneuvering for the Japanese could be and often were a shifty lot whose solemn promises frequently turned out to be groundwork for more extended and complex stratagems to cheat him out of his rightful profit. Herman Fine listened to the radio and cried without tears for the Japanese, who, in an instant of time that was not even a speck on the big calendar, had taken their place beside the Jew. The Jew was used to suffering. The writing for them was etched in caked and dried blood over countless generations upon countless generations. The Japanese did not know. They were proud, too proud, and they were ambitious, too ambitious. Bombs had fallen and, in less time than it takes a Japanese farmer's wife in California to run from the fields into the house and give birth to a child, the writing was scrawled for them. The Jap-Jew would look in the mirror this Sunday night and see a Jap-Jew.

And then there was the reaction of Jackie, also of Seattle.

Jackie was a whore and the news made her unhappy because she got two bucks a head and the Japanese boys were clean and considerate and hot and fast. Aside from her professional interest in them, she really liked them. She was sorry and, in her sorrow, she suffered a little with them.

I would have liked to have a beer with Herman Fine and to talk with Jackie the whore about the hot and fast Japanese boys. The Jew and the whore seem to me the paragons of American manhood and womanhood at that dark hour.

The numbers of the hour line up mysteriously. December 7, 1941, 7:48 a.m. Add 12 for the month to the seventh day and you get the century 19. Add the year 41 to the seventh hour and you get exactly 48 minutes. Our haiku hints at the occult significance of the numbers. They are indeed numbers illuminated by the crickets, which are well known for their aggressive territorialism.

The sadness
of scraggy fields
where we had sat

The whole effect of the haiku rests on the last word. It implies that the speaker is doing the opposite, not sitting down in lush summer fields with a companion, but walking past the thinning green, alone.

The poet Wallace Stevens walked every day through Elizabeth Park to his insurance office. He had married his wife, Elsie Viola Kachel, over the objections of his parents, who thought her lower class. When she showed signs of mental illness, Stevens stayed married to her, but inevitably they drifted apart.

His modernist contemporary T. S. Eliot was a walker, too, through the City of London, to his bank. When his first wife, Vivienne Haigh-Wood, became mentally unable, Eliot committed her to the asylum after a long struggle with indecision.

In its scraggy fields, American poetry is littered with broken marriages. Heartbreak is the making of Americans. Robert Lowell divorced his first wife, Jean Stafford, after eight years of mutual torment, and then left his second wife, Elizabeth Hardwick, and their daughter, Harriet. The suffering of this marriage was given public airing in his two books *For Lizzie and Harriet* and *The Dolphin*. Charles Olson joined Constance Wilcock in civil marriage for fifteen years, and before their divorce was finalized, he was married to his student Betty Kaiser. Denise Levertov was married to her husband, Mitchell Goodman, for twenty-eight years before she divorced him. June Jordan was married to her husband, Michael Meyer, for ten years before she divorced him. Maya Angelou was married to her first husband, Enistasious "Tosh" Angelos, for three years; might or might not have been formally married to her lover, Vusumzi Make; and was certainly married to Paul du Feu for eight years, before she divorced him. Paul Blackburn was married to his first wife, Winifred Grey McCarthy, for four years; to his second wife, Sara Golden, for four years; and to his third wife, Joan Diane Miller, for three years before

he died. Gary Snyder was married to his first wife, Joanne Kyger, for five years; to his second wife, Masa Uehara, for twenty-two years; and to his third wife, Carole Lynn Koda, for fifteen years before she died. Kenneth Rexroth was married to his first wife, Andrée Dutcher, for eleven years; to his second wife, Marie Kass, for fifteen years; to his third wife, Marthe Larsen, for three years; and to his fourth wife, Carol Tinker, for eight years before he died. John Berryman was married to his first wife, Eileen Mulligan, for fourteen years; to his second wife, Anne Levine, for three years; and to his third wife, Kate Donahue, for eleven years before he killed himself. Adrienne Rich was married to her husband, Alfred Haskell Conrad, for twenty-two years before he killed himself. Ume Hanazono was married to her husband, Hisato Hayashi, for nineteen years before she killed herself. Amiri Baraka was married to his wife, Hettie Cohen, for seven years before leaving her and their two children after the assassination of Malcolm X. Lorine Niedecker was married to her first husband, Frank Hartwig, for two years before she separated from him. Philip Levine was married to his first wife, Patty Kanterman, for two years before he divorced her. Sylvia Plath was married to her husband, Ted Hughes, for six years before she separated from him. Carolyn Kizer was married to her first husband, Stimson Bullitt, for eight years before she divorced him. James Wright was married to his first wife, Liberty Kardules, for six years before leaving her and their two sons and for three more years before he divorced her. Yusef Komunyakaa was married to his first wife, Mandy Sayer, for ten years before he divorced her. David P. L. Yang was married to his first wife, Jeannette (Nettie) Nicholson, for eighteen years before he divorced her. Stanley Kunitz was married to his first wife, Eleanor Evans, for nineteen years before he divorced her. Sharon Olds was married to her first husband, David Douglas Olds, for twenty-nine years before she divorced him. For her book *Stag's Leap*, which depicts the breakdown of her marriage, she won the T. S. Eliot Prize.

Tar dust in my nose
after twelve years
still plodding home

When the surface of a busy street, such as Lexington Avenue, has been torn up for repaving, we may question where we are heading. As James Baldwin, who left his city and then his country, wrote poignantly in *Giovanni's Room*: "You don't have a home until you leave it and then, when you have left it, you never can go back."

When the sun drops
another view of Fuji-san
holding up the feet

The haikuist is simultaneously standing on the ground of Central Park and the floor of Mount Fuji. An extraordinary view indeed of both of these places so much painted and written about. Viewed as places for a walk, felt as supports for the feet, they are not so very different. The naturalness of the comparison may remind us of what the Japanese fictionist Osamu Dazai wrote in his short story "One Hundred Views of Mount Fuji," here translated by Ralph F. McCarthy:

> To take what is simple and natural—and therefore succinct and lucid—to snatch hold of that and transfer it directly to paper, was, it seemed to me, everything, and that thought sometimes allowed me to see the figure of Fuji in a different light.

He went on to reject, however, the famous shape of the mountain:

> There was something about it, something in its exceedingly cylindrical simplicity that was too much for me, that if this Fuji was worthy of praise, then so were figurines of the Laughing Buddha—and I find figurines of the Laughing Buddha insufferable, certainly not what anyone could call expressive. And the figure of this Fuji, too, was somehow mistaken, somehow wrong, I would think, and once again I'd be back where I started, confused.

The capture of the mountain's cylindrical simplicity is associated by Dazai with a complacent form of enlightenment. It is better to be confused, to be lost in the vastness of nature, better to walk the ground than to possess it.

Alice Mayer did not paint from observation but from memory. She painted flowers she had seen in Central Park while growing up on

Park Avenue and remembered in her attic studio in Cincinnati, the Queen City. My mother painted fosythia, daffodils, Lenten roses, cherry blossoms, shadbush, but never tulips, the Laughing Buddhas of flowers. Her work always had an unresolved look about it, and after her divorce from my father, the irresolution expanded.

Was it the distance of the past or the distraction of the present that destroyed the integrity of the work? Clients, curators, and critics would find a brilliant passage here and there—the coloring of the grape hyacinth, the uncommon line of the common lilac—but would ultimately turn away with a strong emotion that only later in the silence of a vestibule or the solicitude of a bathroom or the seclusion of a dental office would identify itself as fear.

Alice Mayer gradually embraced the irresolution in her work as her signature, and as a signature the irresolution became insistent and brittle. Her stuttering stopped. Alice in her old age was not pleasant to be with. She never remarried. She hated gardens. The maintenance of the backyard took her away from her work. Toward the end, she kept painting crabapples in watercolor and distilled their essence into a filial series of incestuous sheets. The show won her posthumous fame in the happy ouroboros of artistic Ohio.

They're thinking aloud,
the old zuihitsu writers,
but where are they now?

Is it not of the most exquisite irony that the father of the atomic bomb, J. Robert Oppenheimer, should be so eloquent about the nobility of style?

Addressing the problem of doing justice to the imponderable in science, politics, and the arts, he wrote in his collection of lectures *The Open Mind*, "It is style which complements affirmation with limitation ... it is style which is the deference that action pays to uncertainty; it is above all style through which power defers to reason." We must not forget that you can kill two hundred thousand people with a bomb or two, and also write well.

A tiny leaf drops
into my cup of tea
and then another

The leaves sense their manifest destiny in the tea. The haiku, with its two leaves, alludes to two other poems. The first reference is to the *Records of Ancient Matters*, Japan's oldest written history. Under a huge zelkova tree near the Hatsuse River, Emperor Yūryaku was enjoying a banquet with his courtiers when a leaf from the zelkova tree fluttered down into a cup of sake that a young lady-in-waiting had just served him.

He struck her for her carelessness and was about to kill her when she recited an impromptu verse to the tree:

> From the top branch to the middle
> from the middle branch to the bottom
> from the bottom branch to the cup
> from tip to tip to tip to tip
> falls the zelkova leaf

(trans. Lee O-young)

Upon hearing the poem, moved and astonished, the emperor pardoned the offender.

Our haiku is also a delicate response to a haiku by Bashō:

> From all these trees
> in the salads, the soup, everywhere,
> cherry blossoms fall.

(trans. Robert Hass)

In deference to the Master, our haikuist offers a tiny leaf to his cherry blossoms. In homage to the Master, a cup of tea to his salads and soup. Striking out on his own, however, our haikuist changes Bashō's

widescreen epiphany, cherry blossoms falling everywhere, to the very quiet repetition of the fall of a leaf. The haiku heeds the Master's warning to a prospective student:

> Don't imitate me;
> it's as boring
> as two halves of a melon.

(trans. Robert Hass)

Fall foliage
lodged in a line of trees
cheese in the teeth

When he was designing the sculpture garden for the Houston Museum of Fine Arts, Isamu Noguchi wanted to enclose the garden with walls in order to make it a place for meditation and relaxation. The sculpture garden committee objected, however, to the walls, for they wanted the garden to be open and public. Noguchi resolved the contradictory demands by making the wall of different heights, like a wave.

In an interview for the official opening of the garden, at which Noguchi's friend John Cage premiered his *Ryoanji*, the sculptor said, "As I walked through today, I find the changing relations of the spaces exactly as I had hoped.... I think there is a kind of conversation going on, a very quiet conversation between walls and spaces, people and sculptures. The walls are sculptures as far as I am concerned. They form a geometry of playfulness in a sense."

"Paradise," a Middle English word of Old French, Latin, Greek, and Avestan derivation, means literally "walled enclosure." One can focus too much on the wall and forget the conversation, as Noguchi put it, between wall and space. Focus too much on a line of trees and we fail to see the cheese in the teeth.

What stops me in my track—
an overhanging branch of leaves
the colors of tiger

What stops our poet in his track? It cannot be the fear of being eaten since what he sees is a branch of leaves, and not an actual tiger.

Professor Vital Dove of the University of Virginia is wrong to conclude that the haiku demonstrates our poet's extremely refined sensibility as he is frightened by his own imagination. Such fear, I think, will not be due to refinement so much as to mental weakness. Independent scholar Ryhen Lovable comes closer to the truth when he suggests that the color of the leaves reminds the poet of his past, and so he stops to contemplate a memory.

Pouncing on this suggestion, the Singapore school of criticism points out that a tiger appears in Singapore's coat of arms, which appears on state currency and documents, including the Singapore passport. The coat of arms, adopted by the newly self-governing state in 1959, shows a red shield held up by a lion on the left and a tiger on the right. The lion stands for Singapore (*Singa-pura* means "Lion City" in Sanskrit), whereas the tiger stands for . . . Malaysia. Therein lies the weakness of the SSC argument. They may as well argue that our haikuist is Malaysian.

A far better way of taking up the Lovable suggestion is to recall our haikuist's affinities with Ryōkan Taigu. If we do so, we will remember this charming Chinese-style poem by the Zen master:

> Forty years ago when I was wandering,
> I struggled to paint a tiger, but it didn't even look like a cat!
> Reflecting back, as I release my grip on the cliff's edge,
> I am still Eizo of my young days.
>
> (trans. Kazuaki Tanahashi)

We now see the pertinence of the word "colors" in the haiku. It refers to the art of painting. In recalling his artistic apprenticeship, our expert haikuist reflects that he is still the young man just setting out on his training. The overhanging branch of leaves reminds him of the edge of the cliff he has released.

October leaves
ten thousand reclining Buddhas
open their eyes

What is the relation between these haiku to Zen Buddhism? After much thought, I have concluded that the relation is very similar to that in the work of John Cage. From his *An Autobiographical Statement*, written in 1990:

> When I was young and still writing an unstructured music, albeit methodical and not improvised, one of my teachers, Adolph Weiss, used to complain that no sooner had I started a piece than I brought it to an end. I introduced silence. I was a ground, so to speak, in which emptiness could grow.

> At college I had given up high school thoughts about devoting my life to religion. But after dropping out and traveling to Europe I became interested in modern music and painting, listening-looking and making, finally devoting myself to writing music, which, twenty years later, becoming graphic, returned me now and then for visits to painting (prints, drawings, watercolors, the costumes and decors for *Europeras 1 & 2*).

> In the late thirties I heard a lecture by Nancy Wilson Ross on Dada and Zen. I mention this in my forward [sic] to *Silence* then adding that I did not want my work blamed on Zen, though I felt that Zen changes in different times and places and what it has become here and now, I am not certain.

> Whatever it is it gives me delight and most recently by means of Stephen Addiss' book *The Art of Zen*. I had the good fortune to attend Daisetz Suzuki's classes in the philosophy of Zen Buddhism at Columbia University in the late forties. And I visited him twice in Japan.

> I have never practiced sitting crosslegged nor do I meditate. My work is what I do and always involves writing materials,

chairs, and tables. Before I get to it, I do some exercises for my back and I water the plants, of which I have around two hundred.

My father, a self-proclaimed disciple of Cage, would repeat the last sentence in delight whenever he recited *An Autobiographical Statement*. (He had the whole thing by heart.) When he came to "of which I have around two hundred," he would raise his voice to a shout, almost, in defiance of the world.

He was most probably defying his mother, who never thought well of his decision to become a composer nor of his choice of wives, first, second, and third. Grandma Nancy did not like my mother, but she had a sneaky appreciation of the rebellious streak in Alice Mayer and thought that her son would have been least unhappy if he had stayed with his first wife. The former camp child lived long enough to bury her love child, outliving him by four years.

The Complete Works of John Fujimoto runs to many pages and houses, a paradox for a minimalist. He had a big catalog of compositions and children. It was as if this gentle, considerate man, in appearance short and dark, had to prove his virility again and again, perhaps to a father whom his mother never stopped praising for his matinée-idol looks and who had abandoned his son even before he was born. I have eleven half-brothers and half-sisters of English and Russian extract. After our father's death, we hardly saw one another. John Fujimoto ran out of ideas in 2018 and died at the relatively young age of fifty-seven. Curious to think that I am now older than he was when he died.

From a leafless tree
dangle five long seed pods
all uncircumcised

The seed pods are distinguished, one may say chosen, not by the mark of circumcision but by the marvel of concentration. The end of the sheath is remarkably like the foreskin of the penis. Against the charge of crudeness levied by Konrad Boguslawski and his ilk, we cite the example of Ryōkan Taigu:

The persimmon picker's
testicles look frozen
in the autumn wind.

(trans. Kazuaki Tanahashi)

I did not have a penis before November 10, 2028, but on that day I woke up in Mount Sinai Hospital with one. All my life, my female body had not persuaded me that I was a woman; now my male organ did not so much reassure me as vindicate my conviction that I was a man. It was like having a phantom limb but in reverse. I had not realized until then that I had been engaged determinedly in an act of translation, and now I had the best possible version of myself. I have always been Sam, neither Samantha nor Samuel, but in and of both names.

The pneumatic allograft came from Damian Strange. Although bio-engineered penises were available by 2028, I accepted the bequest of my dead best friend. He knew of my feelings for him, but because they were homosexual in nature, though heterosexual in substance, he could not reciprocate. To show his platonic love for me, he left me his penis in his will, which the good surgeon at Mount Sinai, Chief Urologist Philip Roth, had to attach to me before Damian's corpse turned cold for maximum results.

My mother was just pleased that I had the uncircumcised penis of a goy. She could not stand the idea that Jews are a chosen people,

selected like an apple from the barrel, either for the eye of favor or for the jaws of destruction. I was happy to be uncircumcised for another reason. After recovering his feeling, Damian is super-responsive and ultra-sensitive. He is of a godly length and lordly girth, too. I cuddle the transplant in my hand whenever I write.

Under a rock
a lizard molts
a workman rolls up his sleeves

With Damian in hand, I set upon New York and committed every sex act described in the ancient Chinese medical treatise *Harmonizing Yin and Yang*, dated to 69 BCE. I give the postures below with my commentary in Poundian ideograms:

tiger roving   **^@!)(

cicada clinging   ~&#><?

measuring worm   >+/"%:

river deer butting   =;``;=

locust splayed   //$Xo}

gibbon grabbing   mΣ®ñ||

toad   ¶&_~~~

rabbit bolting   √-------!

dragonfly   ()Ÿ()

fish gobbling   ßOD@8

I even added an eleventh posture suggested by our haiku:

lizard molting m ... mm ... mM ... MM ... MMM ... M m ... m

Believe me, the pleasures were varied and intense, but there was no ejaculate, not a Soylent drop.

The boy in the window
at the back of the school bus
a cricket in a jar

Though our haikuist is not writing a novel, his debt to Vladimir Nabokov is plain to see. A classification scheme advanced by Zimbabwean scholar Derek Attrition is useful here to delineate this literary debt. Attrition boldly insists that all novelists are either deliberately following or deliberately avoiding the legacy of English writer Ford Madox Ford, a.k.a. Hermann Hueffer.

The followers adopt one of four approaches, according to Attrition. The first is the assertion, making an explicit claim about Ford outside of their work. The second is the nod, which consists of an overt allusion to Ford in their work. The third approach is the echo of an aspect of Fordic style or theme. The fourth is the countersignature, which is to rework Ford in some other manner.

Our haikuist might very well have made an assertion about Nabokov, according to Attrition's definition. We just do not know. He certainly gave the nod, as in the late spring haiku "Fallen clumps / of shriveled blossoms," which he compares to "Nabokov's brown wigs." The echo of Nabokov can, of course, be found in all the haiku about butterflies. In the present haiku, our author rewrites Nabokov by turning his butterfly into a cricket.

As Humbert Humbert had his Lolita, Sam Fujimoto-Mayer had his Hermes Brown. The first thing everyone noticed about Hermes was the blackness of his skin. It was so black that it shone. Not like the pinprick glitter of stars in the night nor like the snotgreen shimmer of the scrotum-tightening sea. More like the fecund sheen of a soccer field after rain, in which a cricket sings his jocund song. Everyone loved Hermes. He called to him grannies and gunghos, coppers and cornrows, badchens and betties, pansies and panthers. And schoolteachers. When he picked you out from a crowd of adoring adults— emotional adulterers all—you felt mighty special, as he did me.

It was a moment of weakness. After years of eking out an independent living by Skype-teaching English to students in Tokyo and Tel Aviv, rich kids who wished to study in the United States, I applied to teach in an institution called The Progressive School on the Upper East Side, and I was employed before I could turn around. Hermes Brown, Jr., then a junior, walked right up to me in the cafeteria, stuck his hand out to welcome the new teach, and, before I could say anything half-coherent in reply to his confident self-introduction, walked away with his grinning mates, showing off a rump deliciously wrapped in silky soccer shorts. It was a devastating introduction to private-school teaching.

In the fall evening
green flies glint
mica in granite

In its enthusiasm for all things American, the Japanese art world embraced Isamu Noguchi immediately after World War II. However, that warm reception turned decidedly cool in the 1950s. Japanese intellectuals and leftists were opposed to the government's 1951 peace treaty with America, which allowed American bases to remain on Japanese soil even after the end of the occupation. Noguchi was now viewed by Japanese artists as a competitor and not the messenger of modernism.

His show at the new Museum of Modern Art at Kamakura received poisonous reviews. The newspaper *Tokyo Shimbun* attacked him in the most personal terms. "In Isamu Noguchi's blood," the anonymous reviewer sniffed, "there is mixed hay which is from overseas." "Banana-imperialist, virtue-performative, parachutist-artist," the America-trained, globe-trotting, critical-vocabularied artist Amane L. Kato berated. The green flies glinted in the fall evening.

Even so sympathetic a reviewer as Shūzō Takiguchi, a friend of Noguchi's, expressed deep reservations: "There is something about Noguchi that recalls to one's mind a migratory Ulysses, so to speak, that moves from East to West, then from West to East, then back again to West. . . . His recent works, in medium and subject matter, have become Japanese. . . . Notwithstanding, there still remains something that prevents us from calling them Japanese—something that requires annotation."

Used toothpick
flocculent
as apple cores

A free paraphrase of the Five Books of Moses from Hebrew into Yiddish, the Tsene-rene offers "a verse-by-verse commentary and interpretation of the kind known as midrash—an imaginative expansion on the biblical text," so explains the literary critic Adam Kirsch. This expansion includes not only maxims from the Talmud, other rabbinical sources, and later commentators, but also fables and interjections of the author's own devising.

The author, Joseph ben Isaac Ashkenazi (1550–1625), provided a fascinating midrash on the fall of man. It comprises multiple defenses of Eve. The most imaginative reason Ashkenazi gave was also the most obedient. Since God commanded the first couple to be fruitful and multiply, Eve was only obeying God when she offered the fruit to Adam and gave birth to sexual desire. Without Eve, we would not be here.

Seen this way, the haiku acquires a sexual coloring. The used toothpick, an obvious stand-in for the post-ejaculation penis, not only tastes like "apple cores" but also produces the desirable seeds. This nexus of meanings is admirably captured in the word "flocculent," which brings to mind, and mouth, the words "succulent" and "flaccid." Translation is an original sin. It is also a way to get the word around, to multiply imperfect copies, so to speak.

Manzanar is Spanish for "apple." It is also the name of the concentration camp in Inyo County, California, where Nancy Fujimoto was born. Before Manzanar spelled a prison camp, it was an apple-growing area, but the farms were compulsorily acquired in 1919 and their water diverted into the Los Angeles Aqueduct to serve the city two hundred miles south. And so the valley was translated into a desert, and the desert into a camp. Told that they were put into the camp for their own protection, my great-grandfather Paul Fujimoto asked, "Then why do the guns point inward, rather than outward?"

The observation was repeated by other inmates and eventually found its way into books about the incarceration.

Nancy, his daughter, must have been affected by the shifty sands of her birth in the camp. [Transcriber's note: the word transcribed as "shifty" in the last sentence is slightly smudged. It is possibly "shitty" or "thrifty" or even "drafty." It is hard to tell.] Growing up in Cincinnati, in her father's restaurant actually, she would see her hands dissolving into sand and getting into the customers' bowls of miso soup. Sometimes a customer would confirm her vision by complaining of the sand in his nori. Once, an ample German woman found a big, black grain of sand in her California roll and threatened to write to the local papers. Aiko, Nancy's mother, plied the woman with green tea mochi, which cooled down her frenzied rage.

Tom Park made Nancy Fujimoto a woman, instead of a camp child always on the verge of dissolution. Tom had the looks of the actor BD Wong, as his photos showed, so we can understand why Nancy fell for the handsome seaman. She was also at the same time falling in love with the new political consciousness of being Asian, rather than Japanese, American. A translator in the United States Navy, Tom was passing through Cincinnati on his shore leave. He passed through Nancy's life, too, but not without leaving a baby version of himself behind. Rumors sneaked into Nancy's ears that Tom jumped into bed with both men and women, but she did not care. He died in San Francisco of a disease that was identified later as AIDS. He was only thirty years old.

Three months after he left Cincinnati, Nancy could not hide her bulge any longer. Her parents, Paul and Aiko, were furious. Then they learned that the inseminator was Korean, and they turned livid.

When the baby was born—all ten fingers and ten toes intact, thank god!—Nancy's parents forced her to use the family name on the birth certificate. If they were going to bring him up, they would bring him up as a Fujimoto. Nancy complied, but every night before baby fell asleep, she whispered his father's real name into John's ear. Did baby grow up dreaming of a Park? Or am I making this up because I dream every night of mine?

Big round pear
fresh from the fridge
first ice on the road

Commenting on this haiku, Boguslawski and other critics slip up on the pear. I am convinced that the translation is wrong, that our poet intended not a pear but a peach. A pear just does not have the poetical overtones of a peach.

In a famous Japanese folktale, a child is born miraculously out of a peach. Named Kintarō, he displays phenomenal strength and the magical ability to speak to birds and animals. He is a popular subject of bunraku and kabuki drama, as well as manga, anime, and video games. On Children's Day, not only in Japan but also in the USA, even Cincinnati, a Kintarō doll is placed in the room of a newborn male baby so that he will grow up to be a Golden Boy. My father had such a doll in his room. Born looking female, I did not get a doll. Instead, I made myself over into a Golden Boy.

In the winter sun
a group of leaves glow
like prized marbles

This haiku glows with the luster of nostalgia. Who still plays with marbles? Instead of marbles, young people in Japan have been obsessed with the tiny steel balls of pachinko since World War II. The fever has never abated. Often described as vertical pinball, pachinko was a way of getting around the postwar gambling ban. The odds have always been against the player, not only because the game relies so much on chance but also because owners of pachinko parlors tinker with the machines every day to set the outcomes.

The system is rigged, but that does not stop us from playing, as Korean American author Min Jin Lee showed in her novel *Pachinko* about four generations of Koreans living in Japan. Named *Zainichi*—"existing in Japan"—Koreans are still thought of as transients, if not foreigners, although many have lived in Japan for generations, and some are, in fact, descendants of the 670,000 Koreans brought into the country as forced laborers from 1944 to 1945. It is natural in such circumstances to try to pass as Japanese, as fallen leaves may look, in a passing glance, somewhat like prized marbles.

The leaves have turned
finally
lamp and lamp shade

With ghostly prescience, our haikuist alludes to the limits of commentary, both his words about nature and my words about his poems.

In a review of a critical edition of Adolf Hitler's *Mein Kampf*, Anson Rabinbach puts it succinctly:

> Can a mythological symbol be neutralized by a phalanx of annotations, however erudite? Can Hitler's typical diatribes on how Jews are the "great masters as liars" be demystified with a long commentary on Arthur Schopenhauer and his appropriation by Dietrich Eckart in 1918? As the Hitler biographer Peter Longerich has observed, the method of "surrounding the text with an army of footnotes that would stand watch like a sentinel over the scandalous writ" is only partially realizable. It can also be argued that the annotation—often more than twice as long as the passages they refer to—dignify Hitler's "world view" by embedding his anti-Semitic clichés in well-established intellectual traditions, however perverse they may have been.

After Rabinbach's review appeared in the *Times Literary Supplement*, the white supremacist Willy Schürholz decried his supposed anti-intellectualism in a long, semicoherent article in *Steel Garden*, a new journal published by the Aryan Brotherhood. The attack was taken up by other far-right writers and widened to include accusations of philo-Semitism, anti-Enlightenment, and then, finally, anti-West. As the war of words continued, the annotated *Mein Kampf* flew off the shelves all around the world. The historian Elaine Thompson considered this controversy to be a leading cause of the mainstreaming of Hitlerite ideas in the twenties and thirties. As she wrote, "The bright light shone on Hitler's voluminous tract put to the torch every last prohibition surrounding the hatred of the Jews and immigrants."

American fascists quoted Hitler widely on the race-based restrictions of immigrants enacted by the Johnson–Reed Act in 1924. America stood, then, as the champion of racial purity. Thirty states had anti-miscegenation laws on the books. Why did scholars overlook the influence of the United States on Nazi jurists of the period? They were focused narrowly on precedents for anti-Jewish laws and so looked solely at medieval Europe. When they broadened their focus to racist legislation in general, the influence of the USA came to prominence.

Decrying Germany's liberal citizenship laws, Hitler asked his readers to look to the United States for a shining example: "The racially pure and still unmixed German has risen to become master of the American continent, and he will remain the master, as long as he does not fall victim to racial pollution." Hitler was optimistic about the United States, since in that nation "efforts are made to conform to at least partly the counsels of common sense. By refusing immigrants entry if they are in a bad state of health, and by excluding certain races from the right to become naturalized citizens, they have begun to produce principles similar to those on which we wish to ground the People's State."

Lamp and lampshade, we were Hitler's teacher and we are still teaching the world a thing or two about hate.

After the flowerpots,
the truck will return
for the rolled-up fence

The Lotus Sutra, with a message supposedly eternal, universal, and comprehensive, is thought by Nichiren Buddhists to be the One Vehicle needed for salvation. Not only is the Lotus revered for Shakyamuni's most profound teaching, the text of the sutra itself is worshipped, for each Chinese character is regarded as the embodiment of the Buddha.

Our haiku takes aim at such idolatry. The One Vehicle is downgraded to a workaday truck, glimpsed after a mass event in the park as it ferries off the decorative potted plants. There is wry humor in the thought that a park needs the decoration of flowerpots and the protection of fences.

On this haiku, Ryhen Lovable quotes the very first maxim of *Pirkei Avot* (*Ethics of the Fathers*). The sages of the Great Assembly said three things: "Be deliberate in judgment, raise up many disciples, and make a fence around the Torah."

Of the making of fences there is no end, for another fence is always needed to defend a fence. We wish to protect the Truth, and end by putting it out of reach. If the Truth is Law, *halacha*, how the interpretations proliferate in our judgments and our teachings. If the Truth is Liberty, statue, not statute, how the irony compounds, as we saw with the multiplication of police fences to "protect" marchers protesting agains the incarceration of black and brown people.

Yet it is possible to see fences not as commands imposed from without, but as practices developed from within, to be changed, or even discarded, as circumstances require. This view is hinted at in the words of Rabbi Akiva: "Tradition is a fence around the Torah. Tithes are a fence around wealth. Vows are a fence around abstinence. And silence is a fence around wisdom." The movement from "tradition" to "silence" speaks of decreasing external imposition and increasing

internal development. When the jazz, pop, or symphonic concert is over, the flowerpots and the fences are returned to where they belong. They have no eternal place in a park.

Hot October day
coming down the slope
a lopsided woman

I am almost sure that the lopsided woman is best glossed by a poem by the late-twentieth-century Japanese poet Marichiko.

> The night is too long to the sleepless.
> The road is too long to the footsore.
> Life is too long to a woman
> Made foolish by passion.
> Why did I find a crooked guide
> On the twisted paths of love?

(trans. Kenneth Rexroth)

My hesitation comes from the interference of personal associations, but I would be remiss not to direct the reader to Marichiko's "crooked guide," a close relative of Zhuangzi's Woman Hunchback.

A brown dog
tupping a black dog
an empty parking lot

The first trick I picked up in New York, from a bar in Jackson Heights, was a black man from Port-au-Prince. He taught me everything I know about lovemaking. Gratitude, like a driver's license, is officially nontransferable, but it had an under-the-table means of changing ownership, and so it slipped amorously into the back pocket of Hermes Brown.

He was not in my English class, but I heard all the smart things he said on Shakespeare's Hamlet and wrote on Thoreau's pond and Melville's whale, all the time I was affecting disinterest in his generous mouth or his capable hand. His teacher Mrs. Doris Mooring could not believe that her Golden Child expressed such indifference to James Baldwin, she told us in the office, but under her tone of self-mocking incredulity, one could detect a strain of pride in a student who rose above his race in his response to literature.

As a supportive member of the faculty, I attended Hermes's soccer matches. He was the team captain and, as befitted his namesake, was swift on his feet and quick in his head. I had eyes only for his flashing thighs. By 2043, the USA had become a serious contender for the FIFA World Cup, having come very close to winning it in 2034 and 2042. Football may speak of American uniqueness, but soccer, which is played by so many countries around the world, truly speaks of American exceptionalism. To the aura of a young man reaching his peak in physical perfection was added the flame of national hope.

He was returning from a very late ball practice when I ran into him on the old bridle path that encircled the reservoir. That part of the path, rocky with a thin pretense of sand, had been turned a long time ago into a parking lot. It was empty at that hour, and dimly lit. I held his proffered hand a shuddering moment too long and he pulled me roughly to him, after dropping his Nike duffel bag, and our mouths closed like a vaccum seal.

Oh, he smelled musky and murky. In my nose, the scent of adolescent sweat mingled headily with the odor of dog ordure left behind by inconsiderate pet owners. When he dropped to his hands and knees, protecting both on his duffel bag, he drove Damian wild with desire and heedless of discovery. Dropping down on him, I opened the Torah to expound the Book of Leviticus and taught the eager student that *Genji monogatari* was not the first novel but its own genre.

Red squirrel
carrying off a roasted peanut
quotation of the day

In an article in *New York Magazine* titled "Alien Squirrel," Sadie Stein gathered and organized nuts of information into a timeline that traced the history of squirrels and more in New York. The timeline began in the colonial era, with an abundance of gray squirrels living in New York's forests, one of which Ben Franklin kept as a pet named Mungo and brought to England. When a dog dispatched "the bushy émigré," Franklin wrote a eulogy for it. Stein did not comment on the content or the quality of the eulogy.

Stein's timeline ended with a "tiny, adorable pet squirrel" that attended the Zuccotti Park protests on the shoulder of a Wall Street occupier in 2011 and with an official squirrel-nest webcam going live in Central Park in 2013. Facetiously, she called the latter event the beginning of "the reality era."

If Sadie Stein had extended her timeline to our present, she might have added, for our amusement and edification, the following:

2017
Mustapha Hakkim writes and publishes "The Registry of Squirrels" on Medium, a 592-line poem that satirizes the registration of American Muslims in the first one hundred days of the Donald Trump presidency. A tour de force, written in the form of a ghazal, the poem rings changes on "orange," the qaafiyaa, or rhyming word, and thumps out the ending of each couplet with the radif, or refrain word, "Trump."

2020
While the COVID-19 virus takes over the streets, locking up New Yorkers in their homes, if they can afford not to be "essential workers," the squirrels take over the parks. In August, Mustapha Hakkim disappears from his home in Queens. A witness claims that she saw him bundled into an unmarked van by federal officers wearing the

uniform of the Department of Homeland Security. No one can verify her claim.

2025
It is discovered that the proliferating squirrel webcams are trained on human park users.

2030s
Around the world, the Great Stagflation follows the economic recession due to the pandemic, and in

2036
the first mass protest in Central Park is dispersed violently by the police, killing twenty-four squirrels, more than twice the number of humans. The violence is watched on screens across the country, opened to enjoy the Fourth of July fireworks. It is a black Friday. Over the weekend and into the following week, the police commissioner Brad Wolf parades a series of revelations—videos, Telegram messages, and, with a dramatic flourish, a cache of handguns— showing that the protest has been infiltrated by militant leftists from outside the Empire State.

2040s
Squirrels are dying in thousands because of the Worldwide Drought. CNN produces a well-researched five-part documentary on squirrel thirst, but when the show fails at the ratings, the network pulls it and moves on to more exciting topics, such as Barron Trump's latest squeeze.

2046
On the tenth anniversary of Bloody Fourth, hundreds of protesters occupy the Great Lawn in Central Park, driving the squirrels to the fringes. The *New York Times*, dominated by stooges from the

Democratic National Committee, denounces the protesters as communists one week, fascists the next, and social pests the following week ("Squirrel Infestation"). A bomb goes off among the protesters' tents, killing thirty-four people and injuring eighty-nine. The federal government declares it an act of Islamist terror, although many suspect that it is the state's doing. Citizen videos show plainclothes policemen and black squirrels lurking near the tents before the bomb went off.

2051
The park is closed to the public and Pearl the Squirrel taken down.

2056
On the twentieth anniversary of Bloody Fourth, protesters wearing squirrel masks clash with riot police along the perimeter fence of the park. After the protest is put down firmly, watchtowers with oscillating guns are erected around the reservoir, the watery heart of the park. The fight is permanently knocked out of the protest movement, and it goes underground.

2063
Squirrel meat is sought after again as a protein supplement to New Yorkers' diets once dog meat becomes harder to obtain. It is curious that cat meat never catches on. Since the City prohibits the private hunting of squirrels for fear of new viral transmission, a black market for squirrel flesh and pelt flourishes in Lower Manhattan. A brace of plump squirrels can cost a whole day's wages of an employee of the Department of Sanitation.

2066
Squirrel hunters and trappers begin to notice that their prey has stopped running away. Instead, the cornered squirrel stays quite still, without any fearful quivering, for the human hand or the raptor beak

to scoop it up. The face of the squirrel at that moment of certain death is indecipherable, although a look of despair cannot be discounted. In all cases, the bushy tail of the animal droops like a flag on a windless day, as if in acquiescence to its passing.

It's too cold to walk
I run for the cross-town bus
and miss the ducks

Hermes Brown and I continued to see one another in the park. He lived with his parents and I had roommates, and so the park, the location and locution of our first fuck, became the natural home of our unnatural relationship. Unnatural not because of our age disparity—I was thirty-nine and Hermes was sixteen—but because of the unlikelihood of love across the gulf of knowledge and experience. Yes, love, mutual love, the unmoved mover, the infinite sphere, the center of which is everywhere, the circumference nowhere. I did not think I could love another person the way I had loved Damian Strange, but I was granted not only a time of repetition but an eternity of reciprocation.

Our love was expressed completely (in both senses of the word) in lust. We rambled in the Ramble, rowed on the lake (he sat on me while I applied the oars), and picnicked behind Alice in Wonderland. In the Conservatory Garden I teased him along the entire length of the Wisteria Pergola, he exploded in front of the grizzly bear at the zoo, and I swallowed gratefully under Driprock Arch. It was the very ecstasy of love. We returned again and again to the bridle path around the reservoir, sometimes taking shelter under the cherry trees on both the east and the west sides, sometimes in clear view of the wild but faithful ducks. Without anything as intentional or deliberate as a program, we rode our way around the reservoir, the music of the jet fountain slapping the water always within earshot.

Eventually the school found out (through a snitch called Louis Mutter), the parents went ballistic, and all pretense at progressivism was dropped. I was dismissed, with prejudice, but nothing could stop us. I was never one for institutions anyway.

Hermes graduated, went to Harvard and then its law school; and every vacation he returned, we picked things up as if he had never left.

He had lovers his own age, but he always came back hot and fresh as
a loaf of bread to me.

All the time we fought over politics. His parents were both
Republicans. He could not believe that I would risk my life—our life
together—by joining the Occupy Central movement on the tenth
anniversary of Bloody Fourth. When I survived the bomb blast, he
greeted me outside the American Museum of Natural History, fat
tears rolling down his cheeks, and we locked bodies under the armor
of *Edmontonia rugosidens* on the deserted fourth floor of the museum
complex. Old Rough Tooth was no protection, however, against our
widening political differences. He swerved to the right as I swerved
to the left. When he proposed marriage after he was hired by an
international law firm that specialized in circumventing estate duties,
I turned him down. He never spoke to me again.

The *Times* said that Hermes Brown, Jr., married Wesley Scott Dacy
on Sunday, July 2, 2056, two days before the twentieth anniversary of
Bloody Fourth. It showed a photograph of two attractive young black
men revealing brilliantly white teeth to the camera. It said they had a
direct line to President Barron Trump. They went on to have two
beautiful children, a boy and a girl, by buying the wombs of women of
impoverished means and impeccable genes, and the family, with their
dog, Pooch, became the mascot of the brave new world of New
Harlem.

Moon
in the morning
my shoes are wet

Bo Juyi (772–846), the Chinese poet most influential on Japanese literature, had powerful romantic attachments to other scholar-officials. The most intense of these ties was to his fellow student Yuan Zhen, younger by seven years. After passing their examinations, they both became collators of texts in the imperial library at Chang'an. When they had to separate to follow their different civil service careers, they exchanged intimate poems for several decades until Yuan Zhen died of a sudden illness. Bo Juyi wrote two formal dirges to recite at his friend's funeral and three songs for the pallbearers to sing.

When his friend was living, a poem to him gave us one of the permanent ideas of Japanese aesthetics. In the poem, Bo Juyi told Yuan Zhen that he remembered his fellow student most fondly when he was looking at snow, moon, and flowers; in other words, in winter, autumn, and spring; in yet other words, all seasons. The Japanese took the images to heart and formulated the aesthetic concept of *setsugetsu-ka*, or *setsugekka*.

In one of many poems spelling out the pain of separation, a poem most pertinent to our haiku, Bo Juyi dreams of Yuan Zhen and claims courteously that it must be because Yuan Zhen is dreaming of him. In Bo's dream, Yuan Zhen, too, is suffering from the pain of separation, sharpened by the knowledge that he has no one to carry a letter to Bo.

In the months after my separation from Hermes, as in the months after the death of Damian, I dreamt of my love every night, and was convinced, perhaps influenced by Bo's poem, that it must be because my love was dreaming of me. In my dreams, both Damian and Hermes wept copiously, soaking their shoes with their tears, Damian lamenting that he was unable to revive himself, although he was named after the patron saint of doctors, and Hermes complaining that he was unable to deliver any message to me, although he was

named after the god of messengers. After a time, Hermes began to look more and more like Damian in my dreams, although they looked nothing alike in life. Or did Damian begin to look more and more like Hermes? I don't know. What is certain, however, is that whenever the figure of love appears in my dreams, he bears the glow of the moon and wears the shoes of his tears.

Bo Juyi is more fortunate than I am. He is awakened from his dream by a knock on his door, followed by a real, live voice, announcing itself as "a messenger from Shangzhou." The poem implies that Bo's dream of Yuan Zhen has given the latter the messenger to deliver his letter. When Bo breaks the seal, he discovers a handwritten letter from Yuan Zhen, a single sheet of paper with thirteen lines of verse. The speaker of our haiku is the same messenger from Shangzhou.

At the heart
of the American elm
an old pond

Fr m W ld n by ik , by I n M s ll: "   P nd in Win   "is   c p   I

s lly c s   s ws d n s   nsc nd n l m   d d iving spi i ll ss ns

f m n   l f c s . I's   pl c w   is m s m ic l s b   g   ing d ,

nd w   spi it l s w ll s p ysic l d p s f   p nd,   b k's c n l symb

l,   pl mb d . B   is b ings s g in   m p , c n l   's nsc nd n

lis p il s p y nd   is s yl — b g n lly c nsid d b in ik , sinc f c

s p   f   y g n f ny ik is lik ly   is p cis ly f m i s m   p ic implic

i ns . nd w c ld ls n   , s L k ff nd J ns n   v s wn s , m p   is

p v siv in l ng g nd   g , s if y   sing l ng g , n m   w simpl

nd s ig f w d i sp s , nd b dly m p   is in   s m w . I is   v

n in w d lik s ig f w d , f   ins nc ,   v n in in , in p s lik in l

g g , w ic impli s   m p   f l ng g   c n in . (N   s   c   l ling

is s : I p y c g   ins in   w in   l lin . B i is ls   ik

ypic lly d s ll it c n   sp k , if n bs l ly wi   m p ,   l s wi   c

l ling   n i n i . nd   , f c s , is n   ll   f   , w s   g s   b

il   nd m p —   p i n   w y (nd in n   m p) , w s   g

s f ll w p s f m p   c n b l ng nd m nd ing . c ll J ns n w i

s W ld n is s " s   d " wi m p   i " c lls m   n i n [   ]

nd is m p m king   n i d s   m   i l w   ld " (191 , 200–201) . F

, b k's li nc n m p   im s " l v s   d   d if in p il s phizing

s c d g   l n   l w ld s m f g n ," ning n   l w ld in

li l m   n " v icl f   m king f ll g y ," n l gy , nd symb l " (200–201) .

M p s , s ys J ns n ,   " s lik ly   p k f c l lly c n s c d sys ms f

v l   s y   c nv y f sh m d s f p c p i n ," nd s W ld n b c m s c

mplici in l ding s w y f m n nd s nding f n l p n m n   n

w d i (199) . 's p   y g d s mm y f ll   s ns w y ik nds   v

id m p (l gh   ik   di i n ypic lly v ids p s pp sing   bin y

pp si i n f n   nd c l   s m   lly xcl siv   n i i s) . [Transcriber's

note: the above required careful transcription. The passage is appar-

ently taken from the book *Walden by Haiku* by Ian Marshall, with the

letters of Thoreau's name removed. In Marshall's strange book, the

author extracts nearly three hundred haiku from Thoreau's text in an

effort to prove the aesthetic and philosophical affinities between

haiku and Thoreau. The haiku thus derived are utterly conventional, whereas Thoreau is an original. By removing "T-H-O-R-E-A-U" from Marshall's text, SFM could be suggesting that Thoreau cannot be found in Marshall's book.]

Wind, unpin
the dead butterfly
from the tree

Most Western accounts of the play *M. Butterfly* by David Henry Hwang note the Chinese American playwright's subversive use of the opera *Madama Butterfly* by Italian composer Giacomo Puccini. What is often overlooked is the much earlier antecedent in the Chinese folktale, retold and reworked in countless Chinese operas and stories, called "The Butterfly Lovers."

Like Hwang's play, but unlike Puccini's opera, the Chinese legend involves cross-dressing. Instead of a man dressing up as a female opera singer as in Hwang, "The Butterfly Lovers" has a woman dressing up as a male scholar in order to study the Classics, prohibited to women then. During her journey to her school in another city, the disguised Zhu Yingtai meets Liang Shanbo, and both feel a strong affinity at their first meeting. They study together for the next three years, and Zhu Yingtai falls in love with the handsome scholar.

When she finally reveals her womanly identity because he is too dumb to understand the hints she has dropped, one of the earliest sources of the legend describes Liang Shanbo's reaction, which may strike a modern reader as surprising. In *Xuanshi zhi* (**宣室志**), the author Zhang Du recorded that Liang Shanbo "was disappointed and felt as though he had made a loss" before going on to marry Zhu Yingtai.

Was Liang Shanbo secretly gay and so was disappointed that the man he loved turned out to be a woman? Or was he disappointed because a homosocial intellectual companionship is way better than a heterosexual marital relationship, and so he felt that in the exchange he had "made a loss"? But Zhu Yingtai was no ordinary woman; she was a scholar herself. If he was straight, he could find in her intellectual stimulation, erotic fulfillment, and a promising lineage. And she was likely to have proved most loyal. But that line of thinking is premised on the assumption that he would find a smart woman sexy, not just

smart in a cunning or subtle way, but smart enough to beat him in the Imperial examinations and take a government post away from him, if women were allowed to take examinations and occupy posts.

It is a common enough finding in queer studies that same-sex male bonding often comes at the expense of women. Natsume Sōseki's novel *Kokoro* is a case in point. What is interesting about "The Butterfly Lovers" is that the same person is first appreciated and then depreciated, all because of a change in gender identity. The story, as recounted by Zhang Du, gives the lie to the truism that the "inside" of a person is more important than the "outside." When it comes to relationships, there is no inside or outside; the person goes all the way through, as in the shimmering colors on a butterfly's wing.

Two last leaves
we were awake
and then we drifted off . . .

The haiku floats mystically over the border from wakefulness to sleep, from life to death. It is a death poem, or *jisei*, a genre written to offer a near-death reflection on life's ultimate event. The image of the last leaves illustrates the transience of life. The speaker has awakened to the Buddhist truth that clinging to life will only cause suffering. Finally, in drifting off, the poem conveys the loss of self-nature.

Uniquely, this death poem speaks of two people dying together, like Christoph Friedrich Heinle and Rika Seligson, or Damian Strange and Ada Min Chen, a notion that contradicts the ideal of giving up all worldly attachments. A further complication arises when we consider that the poem is not placed at the end of the manuscript, as death poems usually are.

The tone of the haiku bears great authority, and the source of its assurance lies in the past tense of the verbs, as translator Peter Blejis pointed out. The speaker is speaking of life in the past tense because he is already dead. The authority belongs to one who speaks from beyond. Is he speaking to another Dead One? Yes, but there is the other more intriguing possibility that he is speaking to one who is still alive.

In which case, he is speaking not of death, but of sleep, of a morning, a Sunday morning perhaps, when, lying together in bed, the lovers see sleepily two last leaves on a bare twig outside their window before tucking again into nature's second course. By resurrecting a Sunday morning, the speaker consoles his disconsolate lover who must live on, just as the manuscript continues and does not end yet. The haiku floats mystically back over the border from death to life.

No star in sight
stuck to the sole
a yellow leaf

Here I follow the wildlife writer Richard Smyth in quoting the poet Ruth Padel from her book *The Mara Crossing*: "Trees seem such fixtures, but they were the first great land migrants."

In the haiku, the leaf stuck to a shoe is a migrant, whereas the star stands for a fixed idea about nationalism. Our haikuist prefers light from a yellow leaf to that from a star, whether it is one of the fifty stars on the American flag, or the Star of David on the flag of Israel, or the Rising Sun of the Japanese flag. The light of a star is transcendent but cold. The light of a leaf is earthly, and so it is human. Nationalism, held up as a transcendent ideal, is bound to be inhuman.

Konrad Boguslawski disagrees with this reading of the haiku. He argues that a trampled leaf gives no light at all, and so the haiku points to the lack of any transcendental values that can unite a political community for action. He argues, in other words, for a reading of the haiku as a lament for lost nationalism.

I hear no lament but a revolutionary call to abolish national boundaries. That is the message written on the yellow leaf. As Fred Pearce writes in his book *The New Wild*: "Everything is visiting. Nothing is native."

As well as being a political cry, the haiku is, I believe, also a comment on the art of translation. When I was younger, I used to go running in Central Park. I was never alone, for the park was well used back then by baby strollers, competitive cyclists, and elderly joggers. Going along the inner loop of macadamized road, I would see a runner, a shirtless Tracy Bacon or a crumpled Joe Frazier, whom I would later see running on the other side of the park, and I would wonder how I had run so fast as to meet him again so soon. I knew I could never win the hundred-meter dash even in the toddler league.

And then I realized the simple truth that he had been running all the time toward me. So it is with translation. We think we are running toward the original, to get as close to it as possible, and we forget that the original is also running toward us.

And then he is running past us and disappearing in the distance. All is relative movement and change. There is no transcendent star to tell us where we are going and whether we are getting it right.

Winter trees
in every bite
of birthday cake

When French historian Pierre Nora formulated his idea of a site of memory (*lieu de mémoire*), did he think that such a site might be located in the mouth?

Winter trees
the electrical grid
fails

The comparison of natural forces to man-made electricity is surely older than Gerard Manley Hopkins, but the English poet and Jesuit priest gave it the most powerful expression. "The world is charged," he declaimed, "with the grandeur of God."

The metaphor is charged, we may riff off of the sprung rhythm, by the occurrence of natural electricity in the atmosphere. In *On the Nature of Things*, Roman poet and Epicurean philosopher Titus Lucretius Carus argued that lightning is not a thunderbolt hurled by Zeus but is instead a natural phenomenon. For his efforts to enlighten all of us, he was banned from early modern schools for his subversive views on religion. In Renaissance Florence, violations could incur a fine of ten ducats or excommunication. Thereafter, commentators would highlight the "impious and reprehensible" views of this pagan poet. Even now, schools and commentators trained in these schools work in tandem to keep us ignorant.

When the trees are green in the summer, the Matrix is working. When the trees are bare in the winter, the Matrix fails. And so in this way, failures of the system are naturalized as easily as successes, and the trees themselves participate in our oppression. Rerum becomes rerun.

Winter trees
grow all year round
on the moon

An ancient Chinese legend has a laurel tree growing on the moon. In poetry, the tree has come to stand for something out of reach, a metaphor adopted by the Japanese, as in episode 73 of *The Tales of Ise*, in which the Man was smitten by a lady but was unable even to send her a letter. It is never clear why such a communication could not be made. Some scholars think that it was because the lady in question was the Empress of the Second Avenue, too high for the Man to reach.

In the third verse of the first chapter of the Bible, God said, "Let there be light!" And there was light. Moses de León comments in the Zohar: "This is the light that the Blessed Holy One created at first. It is the light of the eye. It is the light that the Blessed Holy One showed the first Adam; with it he saw from one end of the world to the other" (trans. Daniel Chanan Matt).

My maternal grandfather, Larry Mayer, used to say that God would show him such a world-spanning light and then he would start to write another one of his funny novels about the Shoah. (Has anyone else remarked on the punny fact that the Shoah took place during the *Shōwa* era in Japan?) As Larry wrote, the light would extend his vision beyond the corrupted earth to the extraterrestrial moon. A novelist, he avowed, must be able to see the earth as the moon and the moon as the earth.

He closed his eyes to both earth and moon when he went to bed one night, in 2015, and never opened them again. He was eighty-eight years old. A year before, his wife, the Lily of New York, had died of liver failure. During her illness, he had been a most attentive husband, as if to make up for the years of silence when he would not say or write anything about his parents, older brother, and younger sister who had perished in the camps. A year after his death, *Snow at 5 PM* was published.

Winter trees
fossils from the ocean bed
lifted to the light

This haiku is full of *yūgen*, the suggestive mystery that since Fujiwara no Teika (1162–1242) has been taken by traditional Japanese aesthetics as characteristic of the highest art. The great age indicated in the haiku adds to the dim atmosphere of obscurity. When light is introduced, the haiku stops short of saying what is revealed, just as Shōtetsu recommended in his personal anthology of poems and commentary, *Shōkonshū* ("Grass Roots").

How warm-looking
the graying bristles on the man
selling Christmas trees

In his essay "Meanings in Modern Sculpture" (1949), Isamu Noguchi posited that moden art, newly fascinated with individual psychology, no longer served shared values that were previously imposed by church and state. But he noted, "If religion dies as dogma, it is reborn as a direct personal expression in the arts . . . [in] the almost religious quality of ecstasy and anguish to be found emerging here and there in so-called abstract art."

The anxieties of the postwar years are spiritual as much as anything else. As he wrote, "Our existence is precarious, we do not believe in the permanence of things. The whole man has been replaced by the fragmented self; our anguish is that of Buchenwald and impending cataclysms."

To heal such spiritual fragmentation, he proposed the sculptor as "the great myth-maker of human environment" who would give humanity a sense of order and meaning. "All sculptors are optimists," he claimed. How quaint such optimism appears from our vantage. He sounds like the man who has driven Christmas trees in his van thousands of miles from Canada in order to sell them on a freezing sidewalk in New York.

Hanging from a nail
in the wall of the study
an Olympic gymnast

What is hanging from the nail? A picture of the gymnast, presumably. A model figure hanging by his neck is too horrible to contemplate. The infelicitous translation does not remove that possibility, however.

And yet such an image may recall an infamous work by Isamu Noguchi called *Death*. A naked man made of Monel metal, nearly three feet tall, hangs from a real rope attached to a metal gallows. His legs drawn up as if to avoid the heat of flames, he writhes in sheer anguish. Made at a time when Noguchi was casting about for a social purpose for his art, the work was inspired by a photograph called "Lynched Figure" in the left-wing journal *Labor Defender*. *Death* was Noguchi's protest against man's inhumanity to man.

It attracted much criticism when it was showed in New York in 1935. The harshest attack came from art critic Henry McBride who had already cut Noguchi to the quick with an earlier jibe—"Once an Oriental, always an Oriental." Of *Death*, McBride wrote, "The gruesome study of a lynching with a contorted figure dangling from an actual rope, may be like a photograph from which it was made, but as a work of art it is just a little Japanese mistake."

Also in the show were appealing models for four public projects: *Carl Mackley Memorial*; *Monument to Ben Franklin*; *Play Mountain*; and *Monument to the Plow*. McBride wrote of the allure of these public projects: "All the time he has been over here [Noguchi] has been studying our weaknesses with a view of becoming irresistible to us." The review hurt Noguchi so much that he included it in his autobiography, as if to retaliate, sure by that time that the world was on his side.

On this haiku, Ryhen Lovable quotes Maimonides. In *Mishneh Torah*, book one, chapter 3, Maimonides elevated the study of the Torah above all other prescriptions: "Of all precepts, none is equal in

importance to the study of the Torah. Nay, study of the Torah is equal to them all, for study leads to practice. Hence, study always takes precedence of practice." To which Lovable adds: "Praxis is also a form of study." To which Arthur Arthur adds further: "Take the man down from the nail already." To which Helen Snow responds, "How do we know who he is? May the Messiah not come in the form of an Olympic gymnast? From a *Turnerschaft*?"

A cocker walking
on uncut claws
the clicks of a clock

John Cage once received a request from Enzo Peruccio, a music editor in Torino, to write a preface for an Italian book on percussion. Since he did not read Italian, he wrote the preface not to the book but to the general subject instead.

> Percussion is completely open. It is not even openended. It has no end. It is not like the strings, the winds, the brass. . . . If you are not hearing music, percussion is exemplified by the very next sound you actually hear wherever you are, in or out of doors or city. Planet? Take any part of this book and go to the end of it. You will find yourself thinking of the next step to be taken in that direction. Perhaps you will need new materials, new technologies. You have them. You are in the world of X, chaos, the new science.

When I first moved to New York, I was gripped by the subway drummers who fostered a rhythm from upturned pails. On the muscle of the surrounding fetidity, they inked a persistent tattoo. Then it was over, the tattoo disappeared, and the improvised drums left for who knew where. The drummers gave me an idea for a new poetry, which I was never able to write down. They urged: next step! But I did not know where to go. Until I joined the underground resistance.

Brown leaves penned
in a field of winds
who will open the book?

In the *Zhuangzi*, a story is told of Sir Sunflower of Southunc who asked Woman Hunchback how it was possible that she was old in years but childlike in complexion. To which she replied, "I have heard the Way." Unlike the scholars, the literati, and the monkhood, she did not study the Way, but heard it. When Sir Sunflower asked her where had she learned it from, she replied:

> I learned it from the son of Assistant Ink. Assistant Ink's son learned it from the grandson of Ready Reciter. Ready Reciter's grandson learned it from Bright Vision. Bright Vision learned it from Agreeable Whisper. Agreeable Whisper learned it from Earnest Service. Earnest Service learned it from Sighing Songster. Sighing Songster learned it from Murky Mystery. Murky Mystery learned it from Share Vacuity. Share Vacuity learned it from Would-be Beginning.

(trans. Victor H. Mair)

When writing dominated society and discourse, the way to circumvent and subvert the powers-that-be was by oral transmission. When the World Wide Web dominates, as it does now, the way lies through books, as Booker Fulmerford urged long ago in his sardonically titled pamphlet *Who Wants to Buy a Book about Books?*

Winter rain collects
in the long cracks of the road
and small depressions

Cf. my commentary on "December rain."

December rain
medical records
in a small filing cabinet

The haiku tempts us with a clue to the identity of the insignificant Japanese poet. Our haikuist was possibly suffering from a long-term illness. What was it? The Argentinian literary detective Arturo Belano made a brilliant but wrong deduction by turning to an almost unknown book by the formerly popular Japanese novelist Haruki Murakami.

Murakami was once touted as a Nobel Prize candidate, but he is now read only by specialists on Pacific literature. His nonfiction book *Underground: The Tokyo Gas Attack and the Japanese Psyche* (1997) is made up of two sections. The first, and bigger, part of the book consists of interviews with the victims of the gas attacks and the family of those who died. These interviews are ordered according to the subway lines on which the attack on March 20, 1995, a Monday, took place. Most interesting, and moving, are the interviews of the subway staff who had to respond to the emergency. Their interviews are suffused with pain, guilt, horror, self-justification, and, above all, bewilderment over unanswerable what-if questions.

Part Two of the book consists of interviews with former and present members of the Aum sect, though not with the attackers who were imprisoned or still on trial at the writing of the book. Most members interviewed had struggled with the meaning and purpose of life since young, while feeling alienated from the conformism and competition that they saw around them. They reported their strong sense of relief when they became renunciates and pledged themselves to follow Shōkō Asahara, the leader of the sect, unconditionally.

I knew the struggle only too well while growing up Japanese and Jewish, as do the roughly eighty thousand Americans who identify as both Jewish and Japanese. Not only do we face outright prejudice from the wider society, we also have to confront subtle discrimination from our own tribes. "You don't look Jewish." "You don't speak

Japanese." I am more privileged than most, since my mother is Jewish, a fact that makes me more Jewish in some eyes, and since my father was born of a woman born in a camp, a fact that makes me more Japanese in some quarters.

I joined an alternative community in 2056, utopian but not unrealistic, materialist but not messianic. The underground resistance was a network of cells working throughout the body politic of the USA. Because life aboveground was under continuous electronic surveillance, we limited contact between cells to the absolutely essential. When contact was necessary, we fell back on an obsolete method of communication: pen and paper. When the pens ran out, we made our own ink out of boot polish and brushed our words on homemade paper. We became experts at cracking codes. In this way we escaped detection for years.

My go-between was called Nahman, obviously a pseudonym. I never met him. I was given the name of Steppenwolf. We left messages for one another under a stone at a location that kept changing, by a cherry tree or in a rhododendron bush. To put the running dogs off our scent, we named the movement after a man, the apostate messiah Sabbatai Zevi, or S/Z, for short. A Jewish wit, not me, suggested the name and we adopted it, but we were not following the orders of any one man: we were radical democrats. Any action, whether hacking into the Pentagon or bombing the Washington Monument, arose out of the slow agglutination of consensus. We would have no Messiahs or Führers or Priests or Emperors leading us.

In an essay included in *Underground*, Murakami compared the surrender of one's self to some Great Leader to the surrender of one's life story. "If you lose your ego," he wrote, "you lose the thread of that narrative you call your Self." Turning to the reader, Murakami asked challengingly if we have given up some part of our Self to some

greater Personality, or System, or Order and too gratefully accepted its narrative in return. If our honest answer is yes, at some stage the System will demand of us some kind of insanity.

Arturo Belano suggested that our haikuist suffered from just such a loss of ego. He did not go so far as to accuse the poet of being a religious nutcase, but he pointed to the lack of continuity between haiku, not as a method, but as evidence for the loss of a personal narrative. I concede that there are a few signs of mental disturbance in the poems, for instance, "Winter rain collects," but the haiku as a whole speak overwhelmingly of good health. These are poems written at the height of poetic power; they are not the gleanings of a diseased brain. They do not surrender to a System or a Spirit but work out their salvation with cellular fear and trembling.

Sole dry thing
in the rain-soaked park
an inkling of death

The Talmud mentions in several places a heavenly academy of departed scholars. The Zohar locates this academy in the supernal Garden of Eden. Although our haikuist receives an intimation of his mortality while walking through the park, the haiku is finally consolatory. Nature's deathly hint has been transformed, via writing, into Art's embodied form. Like Rabbi Akiva, our haikuist enters the mystical orchard in peace and emerges in peace.

The choice of the word "inkling" in translation has nothing to do with the informal literary club that met at Oxford in the 1930s and 40s. The Inklings, consisting of such pseudomythic wankers as J. R. R. Tolkien, C. S. Lewis, and Charles Williams, believed in the high value of narrative and fantasy in writing fiction. The Singapore school of criticism points out that our translator Jee Leong Koh was a student at Oxford, a period of time that was described as both an earthly paradise and an expulsion in his poetry. That may account for Koh's choice of the word in his translation but is hardly to be considered evidence for his writing the haiku.

The rain changes
to snow then to rain
the bus is here

This haiku furnishes one of the strongest proofs that the author of *Snow* identifies, at least in part, as a Japanese American. It refers unquestionably to the seminal poem "The Discovery of Tradition" by Lawson Fusao Inada, a third-generation Japanese American, or *Sansei*. Written in homage to two literary forerunners Toshio Mori (1910–1980) and John Okada (1923–1971), the poem seeks inspiration in a distinctive Japanese American literary tradition, not merely Japanese nor American. Part 4 of the poetic sequence is titled "The Emergence of Topics":

> It starts to rain. It starts to snow.
> Whatever "It" is, it's going through some heavy
> combinations . . .

In parallel to the rain and the snow, the section quotes the beginnings of the two works that Mori and Okada are famous for. Toshio Mori's collection of short stories *Yokohama, California* begins with the story of migration from Japan to America. John Okada's novel *No-No Boy* begins with the disembarkation from a bus of the protagonist Ichiro Yamada, who resisted the draft in World War II. From these two beginnings, Inada's poem argues, emerges a genuine literary tradition.

> The rain, the snow, the steady stream.
> The observance of rituals.
> The tribute of tributaries.
> The rain, the snow, the steady stream.
>
> This is how it began, for me.

For our poet, too, the bus was also here.

Heavy snowfall
all white
all whale

Monochrome and monomania: how well they go together! Having lost his leg off the coast of Japan, Herman Melville's Captain Ahab returns to the scene of loss, on a whaling ship fitted with masts cut from trees along the Japanese coast, to avenge himself on the white whale. In his fanatical mind, Moby Dick transcends its own particularities to become a Symbol. Melville shows us the resulting destruction.

Yu Gwansun was only eighteen years old when she organized the March 1st Movement against Japanese rule in Korea. For her courageous action, she was arrested and tortured by her Japanese guards. She died in prison. American poet and artist Theresa Hak Kyung Cha memorialized this martyr in her work *Dictee*. Like Melville, she described the transformation of the enemy from person to Symbol:

> The enemy becomes abstract. The relationship becomes abstract. The nation the enemy the name becomes larger than its own identity.

Knowing her own words would sound remote in the future, Cha doubted the usefulness of her writing, of her remembering. She lamented:

> To the others, these accounts are about (one more) distant land, like (any other) distant land, without any discernible features in the narrative, (all the same) distant like any other. . . . Why resurrect it all now. From the Past. History, the old wound. The past emotions all over again. To confess to relive the same folly.

Our haiku does not confess so much as turn the whale symbol back home to project it on America. The same abstraction obtains: complete, vast, sublime. Like the snow covering the park, it takes all particulars into itself.

When the S/Z cells started winking out, one by one, we realized that we had been discovered. Someone had betrayed us to the authorities. The enemy was within, not just in the network, in the cells of the network, but in the cells of our bodies—the Japanese in the Korean, the German in the Jew, the white in the black, the black in the Asian. In vain we parsed the dwindling messages for signs if they came from friend or foe. We watched in horror and despair as our comrades fell silent.

Our complete destruction seemed unavoidable. It was then I suggested that we write our last testament in the form of a commentary on *Snow at 5 PM*. In this way, our stories would be preserved, not in the priest-haunted mode of a confession, or in the self-satisfied fashion of a memoir, or in the socially agreeable plan of a bildungsroman, but in the combative yet comradely cast of a commentary. Konrad Boguslawski would be likewise entombed in amber. The book and volume of our brain, our testament would be our final act of service to a future society that we are as yet powerless to bring into being. The other cells, all bookish people, took the snowy suggestion to heart.

In the snow
a stone sits on its shadow
a courtier on his robe

In this haiku, our poet brings the courtliness, or *miyabi*, of Heian Japan into fin-de-siècle America. The effect is one of great refinement, another meaning of *miyabi*. The contrasts between the solidity of stone and the insubstantiality of shadow; between the darkness of shadow and the brightness of snow; between the temperature of snow and the temperament of stone: all captured in the first part of the haiku. The second part adds life, from a faraway time and place.

Reading this haiku, we may recall a waka poem involving the love of a liege for his lord in *The Tales of Ise*, written in the mid-Heian period, translated here by Peter MacMillan:

> Long ago, a certain man had served a prince since childhood, but one day his patron took the tonsure and became a monk. As the man held a position at the palace, he could not visit his patron often, but he never lost his sense of devotion and always went to pay respects at New Year. All the prince's former attendants, both laymen and clerics, would also gather then and, as it was a special day, the prince would serve sake to everyone. On one particular New Year snow fell heavily all day. Everyone became quite drunk and composed poems on the topic of being snowbound. The man's poem:

> > Though I yearn to be at your side,
> > I cannot split myself in two;
> > but today my heart's the snow
> > that, piling up,
> > keeps me here with you.

> The prince was so moved by the poem that he removed his robe and gave it to the man.

Sure, the waka poem is not explicitly homoerotic, but neither is our haiku. The homoeroticism, I contend, is sewn into the lining of the robes.

The circle of Suzanne Mayer-Kaufman, the Lily of New York, consisted of many brilliant gay men: artists, writers, designers, and raconteurs. She was fed by Yigit Pura, dressed by Isaac Mizrahi, and photographed by Braden Summers, often with her Löwchen, Penelope. In return, she lavished her patronage on them. Generous subscriptions. Museum shows. Start-up investments. Academic chairs. These men, with their superb tastes in literature, film, and home decoration, are impossible without advanced capitalism. They are its courtiers even when they are its critics.

When Suzanne Mayer-Kaufman died of liver failure in 2014, her memorial service had to be held in the Central Synagogue to accommodate all the mourners. Her daughter, Alice, did not attend the service, and neither did she allow her eleven-year-old son to attend. She claimed that she did not want me to be pulled into the gravitational force field of decadent New York. She remembered being forbidden as a child to wear denim. I think the real reason was that she had never forgiven her mother for rejecting her marriage to a Japanese man. Forbidden to say goodbye to my grandmom, I pay Suzanne Mayer-Kaufman a brief tribute here. *Baruch dayan ha'emet.*

After keeping indoors for two days to nurse a cold, I venture out to the park newly opened since the snowstorm. Walking on snow is like walking on a desert, with the difference that I have too much clothing on.

Sand so white
it has given up the ghost
of a sea

The preamble deliberately misdirects the reader, a deceptive tactic advocated by *The Art of War* by Sun Tzu. What first appears to be an individual illness is really a symptom of race sickness. Not the contagion of the "yellow peril" literally dreamt up by Kaiser Wilhelm II, but the sickness of self-hatred. The word "white" gives the color game away.

After their incarceration by their own government in concentration camps, the *Nisei* (or second-generation Japanese Americans) assimilated into the dominant white culture and gave up the "sea" of their island heritage, their splendid isolation. The camps, most of which were located in the wilds of deserts, were not just about imprisonment; they were also about behavior modification.

In his naïveté, Isamu Noguchi volunteered to enter the Poston camp to set up a handicraft project. To be owned and run entirely by the evacuees, the project would, Noguchi hoped, boost morale, increase self-reliance, and strengthen the spirit of democratic participation. Before long, however, he was treated by the camp officers as if he were just another internee. In a letter to the Surrealist artist Man Ray, Noguchi wrote:

> This is the weirdest, most unreal situation—like in a dream—I wish I were out. Outside, it seems from the inside, history is taking flight and passes forever. Here time has stopped and nothing is of any consequence, nothing of any value, neither our time nor our skill. Our sphere of effective activity is cut to a minimum. Our preoccupations are the intense heat, the afternoon dust storms the food (35c a day) . . . O for the sea! O! for an orange.

Writing to the social-realist artist George Biddle, Noguchi explained that he had entered Poston to "help preserve self-respect and belief in

America," but he had since realized that the government must think "race hatred is good for the war spirit."

The camps converted what was judged to be recalcitrant cultural separatism into the homogeneity of the main culture. To be reckoned to be Americans after the war, the Nisei had to forget they were Japanese. The writers among them returned to writing, but no one wrote about the experience of the camps. The first published writing on the camps was by the African American novelist Chester B. Himes, a story purporting to be extracts from the prewar diary of a Nisei. A while later, the same journal that published Himes's pseudo-diary printed another story about the camp, "My Friend Suki," by Verna Arvey, the Russian-Jewish wife of African American composer William Grant Still.

The assimilated Nisei raised a generation of Japanese Americans very different from themselves. The irony was that, like many American Jews of the postwar generations, the Sansei grew up to despise their parents' submission to the unconstitutional incarceration. They blamed their parents' weakness on traditional Japanese culture, which, to their minds, counseled Confucian obedience. Like my Grandma Nancy, they rebelled against their elders.

Just as American Jews did not know of the heroic young fighters of the Warsaw Ghetto Uprising, the Sansei did not know of the Nisei who resisted the unfair draft of Japanese into the American war effort. They did not know of the Fair Play Committee at Heart Mountain camp, because the only version of history they knew was the version put out by the assimilationist Japanese American Citizens League. So Japanese culture was doubly abandoned. This is the irony so well expressed by the impassioned essay "Come All Ye Asian American Writers of the Real and the Fake" by Frank Chin, anthologized in *The Big Aiiieeeee!* Konrad Boguslawski, who thinks that all

Asian American literature is about a sense of belonging, has obviously not read this combative essay. *Contra* the Squat Tsar, the best Asian American writing, as is true of the best Jewish American writing, is about a sense of justice, the translation of crime into punishment.

So much snow
et written off
the end of January

Commentators have exercised their ingenuity in explaining the strange word "et" in the translation. Is it Latin for "and," as Helen Snow has it? Or North Atlantic dialect for the simple past tense of "eat," according to Ryhen Lovable? Or, as Arthur Arthur argues, the alchemical symbol for ethyl? Could it be an abbreviation for Ethiopia or for international car registration in Egypt? Or an acronym for electrical transcription, Eastern Time, employment training, or extra-terrestrial? Is it, perhaps, a mistake in translation or typography or typesetting? It is none of these. To understand it, we must go to the Zohar.

On the bible verse "*YHVH Ehohim* expelled him from the Garden of Eden ... He drove out *et* Adam" (Genesis 3:23–24), the Zohar quotes Rabbi El'azar:

> We do not know who divorced whom, if the Blessed One divorced Adam or not. But the word is transposed: 'He drove out *et*.' *Et*, precisely! And who drove out *Et*? 'Adam'. Adam drove out *Et*! Therefore it is written: '*YHVH Elohim* expelled him from the Garden of Eden.' Why did He expel him? Because Adam drove out *Et*, as we have said.

> (trans. Daniel Chanan Matt)

The same syntactical ambiguity unsettles our haiku. What wrote off what? Was it the snow that wrote off the end of January or the other way round? If it is the first construction, we may imagine the snow burying or blanking out the last day of the month. If it is the second— the end of January wrote off the snow—the snowstorm, like a debt, has been canceled. There is no snow.

According to Daniel Chanan Matt, the Zohar translator, *et* expresses the fullness of divine speech, as it encompasses all the letters of the

Hebrew alphabet, from *alef* to *tav*. After Adam drove *et* out of the Garden, the language of God became a vagabond, talking to some like the poets, hiding from others like the philosophers, but generally unrecognized.

On a leafless twig
a caterpillar of snow
will change to nothing

We change from nothing to nothing. A meditation on human transience founded on an exact observation. Snow on a twig is long, bumpy, and hairy.

Under the sun
snow falls from trees
losing more of my eyesight

When is a work of art finished? How does an artist know? And if an unfinished work comes down to us, how can we tell if its lack of finish is deliberate or accidental? There are 107 haiku in *Snow at 5 PM*, a magical number since 107 is a twin prime (with 109), but 107 is also in the middle of nowhere; it is not even midpoint between 100 and 110.

The Met Breuer opened its doors to the public in 2016 with a big exhibition of unfinished artworks. I was still in Cincinnati then, an eighth-grader approaching the end of middle school with trepidation. One consequence of having committed artists for parents is that one is lumbered with the ideal of a vocation without an idea of how to find one. Every closing to a stage of life then assumes the coloring and cacophony of a crisis.

Displayed in the last rooms of the Met Breuer show, artists played with the idea of not finishing, having adopted the aesthetic of the incomplete, the in-progress, and the inaction. But these were not the most moving works on show. Far more mysterious and profound were the works stopped, in various stages of completion, for reasons we don't know. They have the quality of works stopped for death.

The image from the exhibition catalog that jumped up and boxed me in the eyes was *Portrait of the Hound* by the British artist Lucian Freud. In the painting, a big white canvas sheet on the floor. On the sheet, Freud's close friend and assistant of twenty years, David Dawson, sat naked with his whippet, Eli. The dog's hind legs were not yet filled in and Dawson's feet not yet given toes.

The first painting that Freud made of Dawson was one of him naked with a dog, too. That painting, titled *Sunny Morning—Eight Legs*, featured Pluto's four canine legs and doubled Dawson's two human ones to make up eight legs and a visual pun on man and dog. Pluto the dog was a relative of Eli my god.

Portrait of the Hound, which is really a portrait of man, dog, and god—a new *Creation of Adam*, if you will—was never finished. Both Dawson and Eli would never walk or walk away. On his last day of painting, about two weeks before he died, Freud was still trying to give the painting all that he had learned about painting. Dawson, seated on the uncushioned floor, leaning backward, supported by his right elbow, had been posing in that awkward position for months on end.

Lucian (courteously): It's no bother to you at all, is it?

David: No, it's about right, I think.

Lucian: You put your knee forward, yeah. Absolutely, absolute-lie (touching his left eye with his painting hand).

The snow unscrolls
for the ancient seals
of children's shoes

Like a seal, which is both word and image, this haiku fuses Buson's aesthetic sensibility with Ryōkan's playful spirit. It is full of delight, or *okashi*, a word that recurs over and over again in Sei Shōnagon's *The Pillow Book*, the first book of *zuihitsu*.

As an artistic medium, a scroll offers a suggestive analogy to the unfolding of memory. A book is less apt. We speak of turning the page to mean making a fresh start. Of Marcel Proust's novel *Remembrance of Things Past*, Walter Benjamin wrote:

> Only the *actus purus* of recollection itself, not the author or the plot, constitutes the unity of the text. One may even say that the intermittence of author and plot is only the reverse of the continuum of memory, the pattern on the back side of the tapestry. This is what Proust meant, and this is how he must be understood, when he said that he would prefer to see his entire work printed in one volume in two columns and without any paragraphs.

Remembrance of Things Past should have been printed continuously on a single roll of paper, like Jack Kerouac's *On the Road*. The novel of memory would then appear on both sides of the paper, the darker marks on one side representing the pure act of recollection, the lighter marks on the other side representing author and plot. To print the work in two columns is a concession to the imperfect medium of a book. And yet, two columns written side by side can carry on a conversation with one another. To recall the past is, after all, to talk to the dead.

Attacking off-kilter
the corner fruit stand
snow at five pm

When Rabbi Shneur Zalman of Liady was thrown into jail for speaking against the Tsar, the prison warden came to him to ask a question.

Warden: I'm told you are a rabbi, so please explain this passage from the Bible to me. It's from the Book of Genesis. After eating the forbidden fruit, Adam ran away from God in shame. The Lord walked back and forth in the Garden, asking "*Ayekha*, where are you?" How is it possible that the Creator of the world did not know where Adam was hiding?

Rabbi Shneur Zalman (with a slight smile): The Lord, blessed-be-His-name, knew where Adam was. It was Adam who didn't know. Do you believe the Bible to be the Word of God?

Warden: Yes, I've been a Christian all my life.

Rabbi Shneur Zalman: And that it speaks to all humankind, of all times, including us and ours?

Warden. Yes, I believe that.

Rabbi Shneur Zalman: In that case, I shall explain to you the real meaning of the question God asked Adam. *Ayekha* means where do you stand in the world? What is your place in the world? What have you done with your life, Adam?

Sam Fujimoto-Mayer: But what if we have no place in the world, nowhere to stand? We had a corner fruit stand, the plastic crates, the weighing scale, the overhead tarpaulin, peddling the fruit of abandoned farms, hell ovens, Tiffany glass, nuclear fallout, adolescent angst, legal miscegenation, war dead, drug overdose, fatal protests, ruthless ambition, bad marriages, seedless pods, and lost love, and

then the snow struck all of it off the page, in a storm of increasing light and dark, not in any kind of clear separation, but in the swirl of ghostly confusion, uncreated chaos. The temporary garden had been there all day long and then it was, not closed, gone.

TELL THE WORLD THIS BOOK WAS

GOOD	BAD	SO-SO

POSTFACE

by Rosemarie binte Sulaiman

It is well known by now that Sam Fujimoto-Mayer wrote his commentary while in detention for an act of terrorism. It does not mean that the work began in the Twelfth Avenue SuperMaximum Security Facility in Manhattan. As his Preface says, he had been working on his commentary for most of his adult life. Still, when he was taken into custody on 4th July 2066, he did not have any of his notes with him. Requesting pen and paper to write his confession, he wrote down his commentary to *Snow at 5 PM* in six days. The next day he was executed by fatal injection.

In addition to being many things, the commentary was a feat of memory. He had help, certainly, from memory-enhancement drugs, which he started taking for an experimental trial at Stanford University, where he was a student. He soon became addicted to remembering. Not only did he remember all 107 haiku of *Snow* in the right order, his commentary is packed with long, word-prefect quotations of a terrific range of authors. With the same facility, he remembered ancient and tribal grudges, fueled by present and personal injustices. The commentary is also a Jacobean revenge tragedy.

Despite the enhanced memory, there are unaccountable lapses. Some are small, for instance, changing the gender of the Afrikaans novelist Vals Crux from nonbinary to male. Other mistakes are more significant. There is throughout the commentary the disorienting confusion of actual people and fictional characters. For instance, Kenji Kanno is a tragic victim of war in John Okada's novel *No-No Boy*. He could not have heard Allen Ginsberg read "Howl" at Six Gallery, let alone have given any kind of smile. And Joe Kavalier and Sam Clay could not have written any books since they are fictional characters in Michael Chabon's novel. Then there are mistakes that might not have been mistakes, not unintentional at any rate. Some passages of the commentary are uncomfortably close to the work of other writers. Are they proof of plagiarism, homage by allusion, or the age-old "committee work" that Fujimoto-Mayer argued is characteristic of all writing, the age-old entry of writers into the bloodstream of language? The jury is still out on this matter, as it is on the ultimate value of this idiosyncratic work. It will be very nearly impossible to judge the work without judging the man.

On 4th July 2066, a Sunday, Sam Fujimoto-Mayer, posing as a Simulacra repairman, walked into the family mansion of the real estate and media mogul Griffith Abe-Zuckerman on Malcolm X Boulevard and started spraying the place with an oscillating gun. Abe-Zuckerman was away on an unexpected business trip. His wife and younger daughter went with him to spend the weekend in Naypyidaw. Only the older daughter, fourteen-year-old Grace, was at home, protected, so they thought, by her security detail. Hazel-haired, gawky, and overweight in photographs, Grace was not the favorite daughter of the family. Unlike her sister, she was not a brilliant scholar at her private all-girls school on the Upper East Side. She did have, however, beautiful handwriting. Her school reports consistently praised her for her diligence, generosity, and friendliness. She and her four bodyguards were killed instantly. Tossing the gun aside, Fujimoto-Mayer then went home, where he was found and arrested by the police.

Upon interrogation, Fujimoto-Mayer confessed, with a slight smile, that he targeted the Abe-Zuckerman family because Jerry Abe-Zuckerman had floated a grand proposal to the state governor to divert the water from the reservoir in Central Park to a new reservoir that he would build in the Bronx. If this plan should succeed, Central Park will be abandoned by the super-rich and allowed to dry up into a desert, as Fujimoto-Mayer well understood. To prevent this event, he had to act swiftly, without consulting his fellow resistance fighters. Needless to say, there is no such underground movement called S/Z. Both the CIA and the FBI confirmed that the network of terrorist cells existed only in Fujimoto-Mayer's head. And no underground commentaries by Helen Snow, Ryhen Lovable, and Arthur Arthur have been found, although that is not to say that they do not exist.

In his commentary, Sam Fujimoto-Mayer maintained that it was impossible for the translator Jee Leong Koh to have written the haiku. He would not brook any of the arguments advanced by what he dismissively called the Singapore school of criticism. As a paid-up member of the school, I cannot help but speculate that a clue to his terrible action lies in his stubborn refusal to credit the translator for the writing. As a creature of translation himself, he should have at the very least considered the possibility. By refusing to do so, he took on the responsibility of explaining the mystery of authorship at the start of things, of locating the original that is free of translation. First, to explain, and then, to act on that explanation. The mystery defeated him.

Singapore, 4th September 2067

INDEX

by Rosemarie binte Sulaiman

The initials **IJP** stand for "insignificant Japanese poet," our haikuist; **JLK** for Jee Leong Koh, our translator; and **SFM** for Sam Fujimoto-Mayer, our commentator.

Arthur, Arthur, underground commentator, a pseudonym chosen by SFM to echo Humbert Humbert obviously; the hermeticism, if it is real, is a firmly discredited approach, xii; social conviviality, 47; eroticism of the blueberries, 135; take the man down, 301; symbol for ethyl, 333.

Arvey, Verna, 329.

Ashkenazi, Joseph ben Isaac, Tsene-rene, Eve's fault, 235.

Attrition, Derek, influence of Ford Madox Ford, 229.

Bacon, Tracy, a homosexual character from Michael Chabon's novel *The Amazing Adventures of Kavalier and Clay*, not a real person, one of SFM's many confusions of fiction for reality; swagger, 31; shirtless, 285.

Baldwin, James, queer writers, 149; *Giovanni's Room*, 201; Hermes Brown indifferent to, 255.

Barzilai, Maya, *Golem: Modern Wars and Their Monsters*, 33.

Bashō, fountainhead of haiku; his name refers to the banana tree planted outside his hut, and so "the fragrant shade of Bashō" (SFM), ix; IJP more aligned with Buson, 25; "Hollanders too," 51; inspired Yone Noguchi, 65; "summer grass," 83; Minamoto no Yoshitsune, 83; poems with an air of intimacy, 87; Alice Mayer's love for, 129; "cherry blossoms fall," 209; "two halves of a melon," 211.

Bee, C. T., *Drop Dead: The Drone Eye's View*, 111; Bee's arguments seem to owe a debt to studies such as Stephen Graham's *Vertical: The City from Satellites to Bunkers*.

Belano, Arturo, another of SFM's confusions of fiction for reality; alter ego of Chilean writer Roberto Bolaño, who first appears in *Distant Star*, leads in *The Savage Detectives*, and narrates *2666*; brilliant but wrong deduction, 309; loss of ego, 313.

Benjamin, Walter, Frankfurt School; unlike Theodor Adorno, did not manage to escape to the United States; Franz Kafka's *The Castle* and *The Trial*, 27; sonnets for Christoph Friedrich Heinle, 137, 139; friendship with "Fritz" Heinle, 137; Skoggard's commentary on, 141; *actus purus* of recollection, 343.

Blejis, Peter, aboveground commentator; verb tense, 283.

Bo, Juyi, attachment to Yuan Zhen and *setsu-getsu-ka*, 271.

Boguslawski, Konrad, Russian writer and critic, xi; the most influential commentator of *Snow at 5 PM*, read by millions, his popularity is probably the cause of SFM's envy and hostility; SFM called him the Squat Tsar; chronological relation, 11; no escape from narrative, 15; HIV/AIDS pandemic, 53; castigates cultural hybridity, 65; semantic fascist, 87; R----- M------, 97; cultural impurities, 147; six pack, 149; pro-Palestine, 167; the 1964 World's Fair, 189; restoration work, 191; crudeness, 223; slips up on pear, 241; lost nationalism, 285; entombed in amber, 321; on Asian American literature, 329.

Brecht, Bertolt, estrangement effect, 29; one of the icons of the Singapore school of criticism; taken from Viktor Shklovsky, his "alienation effect" was successfully rebranded as the V-effect, and then as the Live Vector, and now as OE, or the Other Ecology.

Brown, Hermes, SFM's lover; everyone loved him, 229; first sex with SFM in Central Park, 255; more sex in Central Park, 267; political differences with SFM, 269; married Wesley Scott Dacy, 269.

Buber, Martin, Jewish state, 167.

Buson, the aesthete, ix; aestheticism in *Snow at 5 PM*, 25, 343.

Cage, John, as writer of *Snow at 5 PM*, 125; *Cheap Imitation*, 127; *Water Walk*, 157; *4'33"*, 91; *Ryoanji*, 213; *An Autobiographical Statement*, 219; percussion, 303.

Cao, Xueqin, *Dream of the Red Chamber*, 175.

Carter, Joe, a.k.a Jerry Siegel and Jerry Ess, creator of Superman, 33.

Cha, Theresa Hak Kyung, on Yu Gwansun and making enemies, 319.

Chabon, Michael, *The Amazing Adventures of Kavelier and Clay*, 23; SFM must have loved this novel since he came to think of three of its characters as actual people.

Chen, Ada Min, tar-haired Taiwanese, 79; met Damian Strange, 117; Taiwanese politics, 139; joint suicide with Damian Strange, 139; beautiful handwriting, 141; dying together, 283.

Chin, Frank, "Come All Ye Asian American Writers of the Real and the Fake," 329.

The Chosen One, player role in *Fallout 15.3: A Post-Nuclear MMORPG*, 13.

Chou, Yi-Fen, not the name of a scholar of digital humanities at Columbia University, New York, but a pseudonym controversially adopted by the white American poet Michael Derrick Hudson, x; Hudson was also an indexer, who worked at the Genealogy Center of the Allen County Public Library in Fort Wayne, Indiana, just three hours' drive from Cincinnati.

Clay, Sam, 33; see *Bacon, Tracy* above. In Michael Chabon's novel *The Amazing Adventures of Kavalier and Clay*, Clay becomes the unlikely lover of Tracy Bacon.

Clinton, Hillary Diane Rodham, 185.

Clintwood, Bill, professor of Sexuality and Haiku Studies at the University of New Harlem, 85.

Crux, Vals, aboveground commentator, 125.

Dazai, Osamu, "One Hundred Views of Mount Fuji," 203.

de Grey, Aubrey, SENS Research Foundation, 53.

Dickinson, Emily, still telling it slant, 25.

Disposition Matrix, 113; what SFM could not have known is that the Matrix is no longer discussed by the American president with his inner council, but is decided automatically by computer algorithms, like so much else in contemporary life.

Dōgen Zenji, founder of Sōtō school of Zen; Buddha Way, 87; speck of dust, 173.

Dove, Vital, aboveground commentator, 215.

Emperor Yūryaku, pardoned a poet, 209.

Empson, William, ambiguity, 87.

Fujimoto, Nancy, 1943–2022; SFM's paternal grandmother; "The Dream of Forsythia," 59; hatred of Jews, 59; enlightenment through sex, 63; named her son, 65; Winstons, 75; born in Manzanar War Relocation Center, 173, 235; met Tom Park, 237; gave son John her last name, 239.

Fujimoto, Paul, 1921–1985; SFM's paternal great-grandfather; no-no boy, 55; Fuji Sushi, 59; land bought in his name, 105; mine-mine, 179; guns pointing inward, 235.

Fujimoto-Mayer, Sam, 2003–2066; preface, ix; slanted hand, 25; Camels, 75; met Damian Strange, 77; eleven siblings, 221; genital surgery, 223; met Hermes Brown, 229; first sex with Hermes Brown in Central Park, 255; more sex in Central Park, 267; political differences with Hermes, 269; last testament, 321.

Fujiwara no Teika, yūgen, 295.

Fulmerford, Booker, 305; unidentified, but the supposed title of his pamphlet echoes closely the title of the poetry collection *Who Wants to Buy a Book of Poems?* by Singaporean poet, graphic novelist, and critic Gwee Li Sui.

Gildong, Hong, 163; SFM wrote with obvious identification with this heroic figure, as he did with American comics superheroes and the Chosen One of *Fallout 15.3*.

Gilmour, Léonie, editor and mother of Isamu Noguchi, 65.

Ginsberg, Allen, "Howl," 55; who, 125.

Gizō, A., reverse translation, 125.

Gloger, Constantin Wilhelm Lambert, Gloger's rule, 7.

Goldberg, Rube, Jewish American cartoonist; creator of Professor Lucifer Gorgonzola Butts, 105.

Gospel of Matthew, lilies of the field, 85.

Guest, William, not a real person but a character in a novel about a socialist utopia by English writer William Morris, x; is this another instance of SFM's confusion of fiction for reality, or is he playing a joke on the reader?

Hakkim, Mustapha, "The Registry of Squirrels," 259.

Hakugen, Ichikawa, translator; Ikkyū Sōjun, 109.

Halevi, Judah, the reference to his Kuzari cues the use of the dialogue form in SFM, commentary as dialogue with the text and with other commentaries, 3, 5; SFM ends with a final dialogue, this time not between a Jew and a pagan, but between a Jew and a Christian.

Hanshan, Tang Dynasty poet; probable homosexual relationship with his buddy Shide, 23; "no direction is better or worse," 23.

Harari, Yuval Noah, Israeli writer of popular books of history with pretentious titles; Dataists, 13; consciousness vs. intelligence, 13.

Hass, Robert, translator; Bashō, 209, 211.

Herrera, Hayden, *Listening to Stone: The Art and Life of Isamu Noguchi*, 175; SFM relied on her biography of Isamu Noguchi throughout.

Hersey, John Richard, New Journalism, 121; plagiarism, 121.

Kang, Minsoo, translator; *The Story of Hong Gildong*, 165.

Kanno, Kenji, not a real person, a yes-yes boy from John Okada's novel *No-No Boy*, another of SFM's confusions, 55; slight smile, 55.

Kato, Amane L., uncertain identity; her supposed criticism of Isamu Noguchi's show in Japan, 233, is lifted from a Facebook post by the Singaporean novelist Amanda Lee Koe, who criticized JLK for urging Singaporean writers to speak against the state's supposed blacklisting of writers and academics; was SFM stalking JLK and his circle?

Katsushika, Hokusai, *Thirty-Six Views of Mount Fuji*, 133.

Kaufman, Franklin, 1945–1967; SFM's maternal granduncle; died of drug overdose, 91.

Kavalier, Joe, see *Bacon, Tracy*; comics superheroes, 33.

Kerouac, Jack, *On the Road*, 343.

Kierkegaard, Søren Aabye, highly doubtful that SFM read him; religious vs. poetic response to nature, 25.

King David, the Psalmist, 43.

Kintarō, *Golden Boy*, 214.

Kirsch, Adam, interpretive technology of midrash, 235.

Koh, Jee Leong, 1970–2040; Singaporean American poet; first translator of *Snow at 5 PM*, ix; very probably the writer, too; died from choking on an everything bagel, ix; note on translation, xiv; school teacher, xiv; British education, 15; Oxford, 315.

Marshall, Ian, *Walden by Haiku*, 275; a most suggestive production; SFM's transcriber has no right to comment on SFM and Ian Marshall, but their comment has been preserved in this edition to show the temptation to insert oneself into one's interpretation of a text.

The Matrix, cult movie directed by the Wachowski siblings, 291; first shown in 1999 in cinemas, public halls for screening movies.

Matt, Daniel Chanan, translator; *Zohar*, 293, 333; divine speech, 333.

Mayer, Alice, 1972–2051; SFM's mother; painter of flowers; liver steak, 7; microwave dinners, 9; hard on her people, 43; surgeon general's health warnings, 75; painted for hoax, 129; born on day of Lod Airport massacre, 151; met John Fujimoto, 157; conceived SFM, 159; Central Park, 159; picture books, 169; anti-Zionist, 97; painted from memory, 203; reaction to uncircumcised penis, 223; forbade SFM to attend grandmother's funeral, 325.

Mayer, Franklin, 1970–2003; SFM's maternal uncle; fought in First Gulf War, 91; died in First Gulf War, 159.

Mayer, Jane, "The Predator War," 111.

Mayer, Joseph "Klezmer," 1898–1943; SFM's maternal great-grandfather, friend of Ignacy Jan Paderewski, 189.

Mayer, Larry, a.k.a. Lieber Mayer, 1927–2015; SFM's maternal grandfather; Buchenwald, 5; name change, 33; writer of grotesque comedies, 33, 160; reefers, 75; Zionist, 167; died, 293.

Mayer-Kaufman, Suzanne, 1935–2014; SFM's maternal grandmother; irreconcilable with daughter, 25; marriage to Larry Mayer,

33; Löwchen, 33, 177; Pall Malls, 75; Zionist, 167; patroness of the arts, 325; died of liver failure, 325.

McBride, Henry, "a little Japanese mistake," 299.

McCarthy, Ralph F., translator; Osamu Dazai, 203.

McGill, Randy, forty-sixth president of the USA, 39.

Melville, Herman, Hermes Brown wrote on, 255; white whale, 319.

Meyer, Heinrich August Wilhelm, nineteenth-century Bible commentator; insignificant, 85.

Mihashi, Tatsuya, Japanese B-actor; *Key of Keys*, 99.

Minamoto no Yoshitsune, Bashō's hero, 83.

Mooring, Doris, Hermes Brown's teacher at The Progressive School, 255; did she provide her student his cultural moorings or did she "blackamoor" him?

Mori, Toshio, *Yokohama, California*, 317.

Morse, Rey, nonbinary aboveground commentator; Rube Goldberg, 105.

Murao, Shigeyoshi, a.k.a. Shig, a real yes-yes boy, 55.

Murakami, Haruki, *Underground: The Tokyo Gas Attack and the Japanese Psyche*, 309.

Nabokov, Vladimir, Russian American novelist; brown wigs, 100; *Lolita*, 101; *Pale Fire*, 101; haikuist's debt to N., 229.

Nahman, SFM's supposed go-between in S/Z, the nonexistent terrorist network, 311.

Natsume, Sōseki, *Kokoro*, 281.

New Civil Rights Movement, one of Singapore's proudest products, xii; see *Singapore school of criticism* below.

Noguchi, Isamu, name, 65; on Georgia O'Keefe, 65; Sesshū's "Four Seasons" scroll, 111; Billy Rose Sculpture Garden, 175; sculpture garden for the Houston Museum of Fine Arts, 213; poisonous reviews, 233; "Meanings in Modern Sculpture," 297; *Death*, 299; Poston camp, 327.

Noguchi, Yone, tramp-journies, 65; as writer of *Snow at 5 PM*, 125.

Nora, Pierre, site of memory, 289.

Obama, Barack, plagiarism due to committee writing, 185; presidential inauguration, 185.

Oh, Soon-Tek, Korean mistaken for Japanese, 181; *Tondemonai— Never Happen!*, 181.

Okamoto, Kōzō; Yasuda, Yasuyuki; and Okudaira, Tsuyoshi, Lod Airport massacre, 151; very possibly the inspiration for SFM's terrorist act.

Okada, John, preface to *No-No Boy*, 193, 317; as was done with *The Amazing Adventures of Kavalier and Clay*, SFM invented real-life people from characters in *No-No Boy*.

Oppenheimer, J. Robert, on style, 207.

Oscillating gun, American product, xii, 265; as its name suggests, the power of this ubiquitous assault weapon is derived from palpitations between matter and antimatter.

Ovid, or Publius Ovidius Naso, defended Homer, 65.

Padel, Ruth, trees as migrants, 285.

Park, Tom, 1940–1970; SFM's Korean paternal grandfather; cubeb, 75; met Nancy Fujimoto, 237; died of AIDS, 237.

Pearce, Fred, *The New Wild*, 285.

Penny, Jenny C., forty-seventh president of the USA, 39.

Perry, Matthew C., surrender of Japan, 71.

Peter, a.k.a. Simon Peter, the Apostle and the first pope of the Christian church; allegedly misinterprets the Bible, 43.

Pesquès, Nicolas, writing as embodiment, 155.

Pichushkin, Alexander, two men; Russian American serial killer who murdered his victims by smashing open their heads with a croquet mallet, x; Russian literary scholar, x; both men were named by their chess-mad fathers after Alexander Alekhine, who became the fourth World Chess Champion after he migrated from Russia to France.

Proust, Marcel, *Remembrance of Things Past*, 343.

Pseudo-Solomon, the struggle for Palestine, 167.

Rabbi Akiva, fences, 249; entering and leaving in peace, 315.

Rabbi Shneur Zalman, where are you, 345.

Rabbi Yaakov, appreciating tree and field, 79.

Rabinbach, Anson, editing *Mein Kampf*, 245.

Red Pine, the Chinese art name, or Western pen name, of Bill Porter; his translations from the Chinese were famous for including excerpts from the vast Chinese tradition of translations and commentaries; Hanshan, 23.

Rexroth, Kenneth, *Iliad* in haiku form, 55; Marichiko, 253.

Robinson, Greg, literary historian; on Soon-Tek Oh, 181.

Rorty, Richard, American philosopher; his dubious ideas on irony, contingency, and language led SFM astray; contingency of language, 9; SFM's undergraduate studies, 77.

Rose, Billy, sculpture garden, 175.

Roth, Philip, SFM's surgeon, 223; no relation to the novelist.

Ryōkan, a.k.a. Ryōkan Taigu, moon at window, 81; met Teishin, 117; "All seasons have the moon," 161; "I struggled to paint a tiger," 215; "persimmon picker's testicles," 223; playful spirit, 343.

S/Z, nonexistent terrorist organization, 311, 321; ironically named after Sabbatai Zevi; a knowing pun on Roland Barthes's book of the same name.

Sakura Park, in New York City; cherry trees, 69; bronze tablet unveiled, 71.

Sasagawara, Mari, a character from a short story by Hisaye Yamamoto; one of SFM's many confusions of creation for creator, 59.

Sato, Hiroaki, translator; Bashō, 83.

Schieffelin, Eugene, German immigrant responsible for introducing starlings into the USA, 3.

Schiller, Friedrich, thoughts side by side, 155.

Schürholz, Willy, writer and literary critic, 245.

Sei, Shōnagon, *okashi*, 343.

Seneca Village, 7.

Sesshū, a.k.a. Sesshū Tōyō, school of Sesshū, 111.

Shakespeare, William, Hotspur, 3; brass, 17; incestuous sheets, 115; Hamlet, 255; the very ecstasy of love, 147.

Shelley, Percy Bysshe, "Ozymandias," 191.

Shklovsky, Viktor, school of Russian Formalism; estrangement device, 29.

Shōtetsu, *Shōkonshū*, 295.

Simon, Joe, a.k.a. Hymie Simon, creator of Captain America, 33.

Singapore school of criticism, flourishing center for the study of transnational literature; Singapore's unique culture and economics equip the country's scholars extraordinarily well for the analysis of the relationship between borderless texts and capital; the leading lights of the school are Deepak "Commando" Rao and the twins Aiden and Diane Pong; after the collapse of global oil due to the evisceration of international supply chains by the viral pandemics, the country found "black gold" in words instead; from the mouth of its underground city emits a steady stream of profitable ideas for the exploitation of language, proposals that are eagerly adopted by strong leaders everywhere to create a vision of national unity, where required, or a dream of common humanity; as Singapore's Ministry of Information Science puts it so poetically in its popular Simula-casts, "a word is always more than a word, a word is a form of action"; as for those who still cannot believe Singapore's ascension to the top of the Babel tower, they do not really understand Singapore's strategy, which involves the saturation of all media; school argues JLK wrote the haiku, x; Singapore Literature Festival, 61; *Tondemonai—Never Happen!*, 183; Singapore's coat of arms, 215; Inklings, 315.

Skoggard, Carl, translator and commentator of Walter Benjamin's sonnets for Christoph Friedrich Heinle, 137.

Smyth, Richard, aboveground commentator; Ruth Padel, 285.

Snow, Helen, underground commentator, xii; a protective pseudonym, according to SFM, xii; individual delight, 47; sadness of loss, 131; how do we know, 301; Latin, 333.

Snyder, Gary, American Hanshans and Shides, 23.

Steel Garden, widely respected journal published by the Aryan Brotherhood, 245.

Stein, Sadie, a timeline of squirrels, 259.

Steppenwolf, SFM's code name in the nonexistent terrorist organization S/Z, 311; the 2052 movie of the same name by the Kanda brothers brought Herman Hesse back in vogue.

Stevens, Wallace, T. S. Eliot, Robert Lowell, et al., 197.

Stimson, Henry, secretary of war under Franklin Roosevelt, 105.

Strange, Damian, met SFM, 77; political agitation, 77; Toyota Yaris, 79, 81; New York City, 79; met Ada Chen, 117; wrote poems for Ada Chen, 137; Taiwanese politics, 139; joint suicide with Ada Chen, 139; soap bubbles, 141; pneumatic allograft, 223; dying together, 283.

Sugihara, Chiune , a.k.a. "Sempo," the disobedient bureaucrat, 39.

Sugihara, Yukiko, dream, 39.

Sun Tzu, The Art of War, 327.

Takamine, Jōkichi, cherry tree donor, 69; the seeds of Oriental civilization, 71.

Takiguchi, Shūzō, migratory Ulysses, 233.

Wittgenstein, Moses, formerly Moses Meier, 107.

Yamada, Ichiro (Itchy), literary critic who asks, why starlings, 3; protagonist of John Okada's novel *No-No Boy*, 317; not a real person, another of SFM's mistakes.

Yamamoto, Hisaye, a writer confused by SFM for a commentator, 59.

Yamamoto, Kenkichi, "a critic noted for his insightful essays on both classical and modern Japanese literature" (Makoto Ueda); he could not have "added his voice to the swelling chorus" (SFM) since he died in 1988, ix; SFM obviously wished to enhance the reputation of *Snow at 5 PM* by adducing a dead man's voice.

Yeats, William Butler, "monuments of unageing intellect," 17.

Zappa, *We're Only in It for the Money*, 91.

Zevi, Sabbatai, 1626–1676; claimed to be the Jewish messiah and founded the Sabbatean movement, 311.

Zhang, Du, *Xuanshi zhi*, 279.

Zhuangzi, Woman Hunchback, 131, 253, 305.

Zohar, *neshamah*, 131; first light, 293; academy of dead scholars, 315; "We do not know who divorced whom," 333.

Zoilus the Homeromastix, Scourge of Homer, 67.

Zubieta, Ignacio, not a real person, but a character in *Nazi Literature in the Americas* by Roberto Bolaño, 149.

DEDICATION AND CREDITS

Snow at 5 PM owes an immense debt to many writers, translators, commentators, biographers, and thinkers, listed here in a somewhat quixotic attempt at a ranked order of importance to the writing of this work:

- Vladimir Nabokov, Bashō-Buson-Issa, Elie Wiesel, John Okada, Moses, Lady Murasaki, Herman Hesse, Roberto Bolaño, Walt Whitman, Ryōkan Taigu, William Shakespeare, Yone Noguchi, the author of *Ise monogatari*, Ikkyū Sōjun, King David, Saint Luke, Franz Kafka, Hisaye Yamamoto, Lawson Fusao Inada, Toshio Mori, the author of *Heike monogatari*, Bo Juyi, Judah Halevi, Michael Chabon, Henry David Thoreau, the author of *Hong Gildong jeon*, Herman Melville, Theresa Hak Kyung Cha, John Richard Hersey, Kenneth Rexroth, Hanshan, Allen Ginsberg, Zappa, Haruki Murakami, Soon-Tek Oh, Osamu Dazai, Min Jin Lee, David Henry Wang, Woody Allen, Richard Smyth, Ruth Padel, Marcus Aurelius, Natsume Sōseki, T. S. Eliot et al., James Baldwin, Oscar Wilde, Cao Xueqin, Ishikawa Takuboku, Walther von der Vogelweide, William Carlos Williams, Friedrich Schiller, Percy Bysshe Shelley, Amanda Lee Koe, Lucretius, Horace, Ovid, Gerard Manley Hopkins, W. B. Yeats, Gwee Li Sui, Sei Shōnagon, Emily Dickinson, Robert Frost, Marcel Proust, Jack Kerouac, Chester B. Himes, Verna Arvey, Sadie Stein,

- W. S. Merwin and Takako Lento, Kazuaki Tanahashi, Daniel Chanan Matt, Peter MacMillan, Victor H. Mair, Red Pine,

Hiroaki Sato, Ichikawa Hakugen, Minsoo Kang, Ralph F. McCarthy, Robert Hass, Arthur Waley, Ivan Morris,

- Makoto Ueda, Walter Benjamin, Lee O-young, Adam Kirsch, Samuel Taylor Coleridge, the authors of *Pirkei Avot*, Maimonides, Jacob ben Isaac Ashkenazi, Henry Abelove, Frank Chin, Carl Skoggard, William Empson, Isaac M. Wise, Ian Marshall, Heinrich August Wilhelm Meyer, Moses de León, Dajian Huineng, Fujiwara no Teika, Shōtetsu, Bertolt Brecht, Viktor Shklovsky, Maya Barzilai, Roland Barthes, Nicolas Pesquès, Hal Jensen, Greg Robinson,

- Hayden Herrera, Amy Sueyoshi, Gershom Scholem, Kai Bird, Martin J. Sherwin,

- Zhuangzi, Richard Rorty, Frantz Fanon, the author of the Zohar, Dōgen Zenji, Gillian Rose, Yuval Noah Harari, Michi Weglyn, Anson Rabinbach, J. Robert Oppenheimer, Sun Tzu, Ludwig Wittsgenstein, Søren Aabye Kierkegaard, and Pierre Nora.

My reading was supplemented and influenced by research in Wikipedia; *Times Literary Supplement*; *New York Times*; *New Yorker*; *New York Magazine*; the online Stanford Encyclopedia of Philosophy; *A Sourcebook in Asian Philosophy*, ed. John M. Koller and Patricia Koller; *Two-Timing Modernity: Homosocial Narrative in Modern Japanese Fiction*, by J. Keith Vincent; *The Columbia Anthology of Japanese Essays: Zuihitsu from the Tenth to the Twenty-First Century*, ed. and trans. Steven D. Carter; *The People and the Books: 18 Classics of Jewish Literature*, by Adam Kirsch; *The Cambridge Companion to Asian American Literature*, ed. Crystal Parikh and Daniel Y. Kim; *A Maimonides Reader*, ed. Isadore Twersky; *Introduction to German Poetry*, ed. Gustave Mathieu and Guy Stern; *Zen Landscapes:*

Perspectives on Japanese Gardens and Ceramics, by Allen S. Weiss; and *Zen Spaces and Neon Places: Reflections on Japanese Architecture and Urbanism*, by Vinayak Bharne.

This work of fiction is dedicated to Jin Hirata, who left us too soon on September 4, 2016. Jin loved Central Park and started every day—rain, snow, or shine—with a long walk there. Whether he was photographing a red-tailed hawk or a lilac shrub in bloom, he saw in the park every good thing about New York City and the USA, to which he moved with such high hopes from Japan and Singapore. He also loved a good political debate.

My deep gratitude to my dear friends Andrew Howdle, Helaine Smith, and Henry Abelove for reading and responding to this and other work. Your comments made me think harder about what this book could and should be. You may or may not recognize yourselves in this book.

Big thanks to Eric Norris for recommending Nabokov so enthusiastically and reading an early draft of this manuscript. Ray Briggs and Ying Sze Pek perceptively questioned the dubious philosophical and artistic ideas in the book. Kimberley Lim was my superb copy editor who saved me from one thousand and one errors. And, always, my love to Guy E. Humphrey, who read this work and urged me to make it longer.

PERMISSIONS

AUTHOR'S BIOGRAPHY

Jee Leong Koh is the author of *Steep Tea* (Carcanet), named as one of the best books of 2015 by UK's *Financial Times* and a finalist in the Lambda Literary Awards in the US. He has published four other books of poetry, a volume of essays, and a collection of zuihitsu. His work has been translated into Japanese, Chinese, Malay, Vietnamese, Russian, and Latvian. Originally from Singapore, he lives in New York, where he heads the literary nonprofit Singapore Unbound and the indie press Gaudy Boy.

Other books by Jee Leong Koh:

Poetry
Payday Loans (Poets Wear Prada Press)
Equal to the Earth (Bench Press)
Seven Studies for a Self Portrait (Bench Press)
Steep Tea (Carcanet Press)
Connor & Seal (Sibling Rivalry Press)

Essays
Bite Harder: Open Letters and Close Readings (Ethos Books)

Zuihitsu
The Pillow Book (Math Paper Press)
The Pillow Book: English-Japanese Illustrated Edition (Awai Books)

CPSIA information can be obtained
at www.ICGtesting.com
Printed in the USA
FSHW010507150920
73800FS